UNFORGETTABLE MEMORIES

A NOVEL

PON KULENDIREN

Contents

Contents

Foreword

This Novel is an unusual one, as it is more or less a history book in the form of a novel with details of villages, many temples, and places of importance in the Jaffna peninsula, the northern part of Sri Lanka.

The hero of the novel Dr. Jeevan from Canada is visiting his native place Chunnakam after four decades. He is seeing the gradual changes in his birthplace and the surrounding villages and was amazed, astonished, and at the same time overcome with sadness. He was able to witness the damages done to these places during the Civil war, which lasted for three decades. He made it a point to visit the places he had seen during his school days and meet his teachers, friends, and acquaintances, who were there.

Every chapter of this novel depicts the past and the present status of these people and places. A person who had his roots in Jaffna would be able to visualize and connect to the events and places described in the novel. To a stranger, they may look funny and surprising. Most of the places and the houses in the area where he was born and bred, looked new and he was not able to recognize them. He could see the people and places have undergone a vast transformation.

Death and destruction brought by the Civil War caused sympathy, suffering, and anguish in his mind. He was able to picture the past situation of these places, during his school days and was able to compare their present pathetic state. He visited Jaffna to establish a Seniors home on his ancestral property and was able to achieve his aim with the help of a lawyer Rajan.

FOREWORD

This Novell contains vivid descriptions of Sri Lanka's Colonial history of 450 years by the Portuguese, Dutch end the British. Many milestone events during this period have been described in detail. Hence, I have a feeling that the author must have done extensive research from various resources to collect all these valuable data.

This novel also contains interesting details about the people of the area, the nature of the social strata, and their lives of them in those days. These may be shocking details for people, who are not used to the customs and old traditions of the Tamil people.

Some of these details and events are repeated in two or three places in the novel, which appear to be redundant and could have been avoided. The author cleverly brings in the love affair of the hero during his school days and made it a point to meet them after 40 years, to reminisce on their romantic past. This adds flavor to the novel and makes it interesting.

Overall, this novel with many historical facts may be an interesting read for Sri Lankan expatriates and history lovers in general.

The author has published many novels, a collection of short stories, and articles on science, Tamil culture, and history in Tamil and English.

Some of his books have won awards and accolades and I wish him well in his future endeavors.

Siva Sinniah
Asst. Professor, Annamalai Canada Campus
Emeritus Principal, Kopay Christian College, Sri Lanka.

Preface

This novel, with the title Unforgettable Memories, is the story of the changes in a village before 1948 and after the independence of Sri Lanka. The village in this novel is a farming village Chunnakam which is in the Valigamam division in northern Sri Lanka. Chunnakam is one of the farming villages in the Jaffna Peninsula on the island of Sri Lanka. The old name of Chunnakam was Milani. Many years ago, Peacocks roamed in the forest in that area. Chunnakam is a village located in the middle of the peninsula, at the sixth-mile post from Jaffna town, on the road to Kankesanthurai port. Chunnakam village is bounded on the north by Mallakam, on the south by Uduvil, on the west by Kandarodai, and on the east by Punnalaikattuvan.

The village is in the middle of important agricultural areas and is also a hub for special agricultural services. The market for vegetables and agricultural products located here is popular in the region.

There are five areas namely Vadamartachi. Thenmaratchi, Valikamam North, Valikamam south, and Islands in Jaffna Peninsula. This novel covers the Valikamam South area where Caste, religion, education, traditions, politics, beliefs, and natural resources prevailed as in other areas in Jaffna Peninsula.

The novel focuses on the Scio Economic aspects of the Chunnakam village and its surrounding villages in Valikamam.

The novel centers around a man who was born and raised in the village of Chunnakam and worked as a doctor in the Sri Lankan government for a few years, and after that. emigrated to Canada due to ethnic riots.

In Canada, he married a Malaysian Tamil woman and had a son and a daughter. He lived there for more than forty years, without returning to the village where he was born. Due to the Eelam war, he could not attend his parents' funeral and do his traditional rights. After more than four decades, to sort out the legal issues associated with his parent's land, he returns to the village he was born.

During his school days, he played cricket with his friends, studied in a college, and entered medical college. During his school days, he loved a pretty girl from his village, who was the sister of his friend.

The novel investigates social, economic, traditional, and political changes in the village. When he met the people who survived the war, he recalls his old memories.

The novel also narrates the story of how his father who got the title of Mudaliyar, when worked in the government Kachcheri Administrative officer under the British government. The government agent of the Northern province was a Britisher who was called Rajah of Jaffna .during the British rule. The father of the hero of the story was a well-respected man in the village who contributed to the development of the village and helped the poor villagers. During his return to the village, he was guided by his family lawyer. In this story, the man who came to town meets the woman he fell in love with during his school days. the novel explains what transpired between them.

On his return journey to Canada, he spends three days in Colombo, meeting the Professors who taught him at the medical college. He happened to meet a three-wheel driver who gives his view about how the country has changed after the independence.

The novel was written from a slightly different point of view to depict the changes that are taking place in the villages in the Northern province and the part played by the expatriate Tamil population. It identifies the reasons for the changes and heritage sites available in the Northern province.

Thanks

****

CHAPTER ONE

THE LETTER

Dr. Jeevan lives in Richmond Hill, Ontario Canada. He is the son of Late Mudaliyar Murugesu of Chunnakam, a village in the Jaffna peninsula.

It was a Saturday. Jeevan after having cornflake cereals with milk, green tea, and peach for the morning breakfast was watching the CBC news. The news reporter announced that the Ontario government relaxed the rule of wearing masks. The news reporter also announced the fourth dose of the Covid 19 vaccination can be done in drug stores.

The doorbell rang. Jeevan went and opened the door. DHL courier delivered a letter. He signed and took over the letter. The letter was from his family lawyer Rajan from his village Chunnagam in the Northern province of Sri Lanka.

He opened and read the letter. His wife Malini and two children were listening to the letter being read out.

" My dear Dr. Jeevan

I am Rajendran (Rajan) your parent's family lawyer. How are you and your family keeping? You may be surprised to receive this urgent letter from me from Chunnagam the village in Valigamam where you were born. You are aware that I am a relation of your father Mudaliar Murugesu. I am writing this urgent letter as it is time for you to come to the Village to sort out the legal issues of the will written in your name by your father and mother. The Two-acre land and the house written in your name are in pathetic condition. There is all possibility that intruders may occupy your land and use the well that contains good water. After that, it will be exceedingly difficult to eject them. Please come with a plan for how you are going to use the damaged house and the neglected land.

Please reply to me with the date and time of your arrival in Colombo and Chunnagam. I will make hotel arrangements for your stay in Colombo and Chunnagam. My lawyer friend Alwis will meet you at the Bandaranaike International Airport. In your reply indicate whether you are coming with your family. My email is Rajan1935@gmail.com

Dr. Jeevan knew that Uncle Rajan was five years elder than him as he has given his year of birth as 1935 in his email ID.

Jeevan's wife Malini works as a nurse in a hospital in Markham. He met her a few years after arriving in Canada when he started working in Markham health network hospital. Jeevan liked Malini, fell in love with her, and married her. They had a son by the name of Ramesh and a daughter Devy, both are now working. All this happened after he arrived in Canada from Sri Lanka more than forty years ago. Jeevan never had the opportunity to go back to his village because of the war in the Northern and Eastern provinces. Although he was the only child of his parents, he could not attend their funerals and do the Hindu funeral rituals.

After listening to the letter read out by her husband, Malini said

"So, Jeevan what have you decided ?"

"Well, I must go to my Village otherwise my ancestral house and land will encroach. Sometimes the Town council may take over that land. I want to sort out things regarding the will written by my parents ."

" What are you going to do with that house and the land? Are you going to sell it? Our family is not going back to that village. We are Canadian citizens. Do you have any plan ?" Malini asked her husband.

" Yes, I have a plan to start a Seniors Home in that house. I have already discussed with some associations run by people from villages in Valigamam. They agreed to support me."

"I know some time back you mentioned starting a Senior home in your ancestral

" Malini, we have here many societies formed by those who lived in Villages such as Innuvil, Uduvil, Manipay, Alavetty, Kupilan, and Mallakam. I spoke to the Board of directors of those societies, and they welcome my idea and promised to financially support the Project. They asked me to go to my village and initiate action on the project."

" I know that you were the president of Chunnkam Canada Association for four years and now continuing as their advisor. You also have close contact with your Skandvordaya college old boy's association. I am certain that they will support you on the project," Malini said.

" Yes, we as expatriate Tamils only can help to develop the villages where we

" I like your plan to help the people in the villages.

I have no objection to you going to that beautiful country. A long time ago when I was ten years old, I went to my father's village in Urimpirai. He was born in that village, but he worked in Malaysia as a station master during British rule and later married my mother Meenatchi from Tamil

Naadu. I am not too sure about the political, security, and economic condition of the country. Since you can speak English, Tamil and Sinhalese you can easily manage any situation there.

" True Malini, I learned to read and speak Sinhalese, because I worked as a doctor in Singhalese areas. I never worked in the Northern or Eastern provinces."

Jeevan's son Ramesh and daughter Devi, we were listening to the parent's conversation.

Ramesh said, " Dad I would like to join you and come and assist you in your project. I and my sister love to see our ancestral house and village, unfortunately, I have started work in my marketing Consultancy organization only a few months ago and I am sure they will not give me leave until I complete one year of service with them. That was the condition when they employed me."

" Do not worry Ramesh. I will sort out things on legal matters and get the ball rolling after that you and your sister may follow up on the project after one year. I know a lady there who may if she agrees will oversee the Senior's home that will start in our ancestral property."

"That's a clever idea Dad, but I am also doing my master's degree at York University, and I must complete it by next year after that I will be ready to go next year with my brother, mother, and you and see how far your project progressed and give a helping hand. As my brother said I love to see the village where you were born. I had a look at it in Google Maps. It looks like the village is located near an Airport and Harbor," Devi said.

" True Devi. The Airport is called Palaly airport. It was built by the British before Independence. The Harbor is called Kankesanthurai harbor. There is a legendary story behind its name."

" If things are okay in Sri Lanka, Jeevan, we will go to Sri Lanka as a family next year. I too want to show my children the Urimpirai village where my father was born."

" Melani, Urimpirai village is not too far from Chunnagam. Many Malayan pensioners lived there. This is what my mother once told me. Her father too was a Malayan pensioner."

" Is that so. I am happy to hear that. Sometimes my father was related to your mother's father. Who knows?"

Malini now I will reply to Uncle Rajan about our family decision. I will write to him saying that I will be coming to Chunnakam alone to sort out the legal aspects of my property and give a kick start for my Senior home project. I will go on one month's leave. It is a good opportunity for me to see how my villages in Valigamam have changed. It is more than forty years. After the war, many people lost their dear ones. There was a genocide in Vanni and Chunnakam markets. The government is trying to cover it up. UN is passing resolutions after resolutions. I love the people and teachers who I knew when I was a student. I may visit my college from where I entered medical college. Some of the class mares may be living in that village. There was Krishnan who competed with me in my studies. There was my close friend Ravi with whom I played cricket. We both went to Jaffna to watch Tamil movies. I want to see the Chunnakam market that was built by the Dutch more than two hundred years ago. I went to Keerimalai when Ravi taught me to Swim.

I wish to see my professors in Colombo and see how far Colombo has changed. I will never forget the riots that took place in areas where Tamils lived. After leaving that country about four decades ago I will be meeting my old friend Dr. Rashid from Kurunegala. I went to his house once and had Biryani and Wattalappamn. His father was a businessperson. I knew that Dr. Rashid had a political issue and was in remand Jail for a year on false complaints. Political vindictive activities are quite common in Sri Lanka. That is why I avoided taking politics when I worked there. I heard that he was released six months ago without any charges. He was interdicted based on false complaints."

" Dad the Sri Lankan Singhala politicians are so vindictive. There is a Sinhalese friend who is working. He told his father who was working as a Senior Engineer complained to the Bribery commission about his minister who was taking bribes on the highway project. No action was taken. He found it difficult to work in the department. He was overlooked for the promotion that he was to get. Si his father migrated to Canada."

"Okay, children let us not talk about Sri Lankan politics. Many Canadians are aware that it is a country that excels in corruption, violence, and human rights violations. I read in the newspaper that there are protests all over the country as the cost of living has gone up.

Jeevan that is a good decision to go to your village and sort out the will and see your old friends. Avoid getting involved in politics or demonstrations. I will get the tickets booked for you and pack things ready for your travel. Now that you have a few years to retire, you will have no problem getting leave. You have taken all four COVI 19 Vaccinations and have the certificates. It is important in Sri Lanka that you have those documents. Take your Sri Lankan ID card with you." Malini advised her husband.

" Daddy please bring me s devil mask. I saw one in a Sri Lankan restaurant" Devi said,

" Devi your dad is not going to Sri Lanka to do shopping. Do not ask him to buy things," Malini said to her daughter.

****

After booking the tickets Jeevan replied by email to the lawyer Rajan about the date and time of his arrival in Sri Lanka and requested him to book the hotel in Colombo and Chunnakam.

Before leaving Canada, Jeevan contacted some village associations and his school old boy's association and informed them about his trip to Chunnakam. They blessed him with success on his project and promised him support for the project. They also advised him to avoid talking about politics and his views about the government.

*****

CHAPTER TWO

THE AIR LANKA FLIGHT

Before leaving Toronto Paterson Airport, Jeevan promised his wife that he will be in constant contact with the family and keep them informed of the situation in his village and Sri Lanka.

His flight to London was a six-hour flight on Air Canada. Another two-hour transit in London, then an eight-hour direct flight to Colombo on Air Lanka. He remembered the flight he took to London by British Airways via Teheran and then by Air Canada from London to Toronto when he migrated to Canada forty years ago. At that time when he landed in Toronto in December, it was snowing. That was the first time he saw snow. Before he left for Canada, he was advised by his friends to wear warm clothes to meet the wintry weather. His medical college friend Dr. Roopan was there at the airport to meet him. Dr. Roopan migrated two years before Jeevan. Jeevan stayed with him for a few months until he found his accommodation.

' On the Air Canada flight to London, Jeevan met three families who were traveling to Colombo.

Two families were Tamils from the Northern province, and the third family was a Sinhalese family from Galle, a city in the Southern part of Sri Lanka.

Jeevan had a chance to speak to them. He found that two Tamil families migrated after the 1977 communal riots when many Tamil houses in Colombo were burnt.

One Tamil family was from Point Pedro and the other family was from Colombo. The third Singhala family came to Canada because they were politically victimized after the election. Dr. Jeevan did not want to ask the Singhalese family further questions as it was personal, and they may not tell him the truth.

After two hours of transit in London Jeevan took the Air Lanka flight from London to Colombo/ Two English passengers occupied the two seats next to Jeevan's seat. After the flight took off for its eight-hour final part of the journey to Colombo. Both passengers introduced themselves as Dr. James Watson and Mr. John Ward. Jeevan introduced him as Dr. Murugesu Jeevan, the son of Mudaliyar Murugesu.

Both Englishmen were traveling as tourists to see the tombs of their ancestors who died in Sri Lanka.

James Watson informed Jeevan that he is the great-grandson of James Taylor from Scotland who had the first tea plantation in Sri Lanka in the 19th century. He said that he is visiting Sri Lanka as he is anxious to see the Tea estate his great grandfather from Scotland started and the bungalow where he lived. He also asked Jeevan what the Mudaliyar title means.

"Mr. Watson, the titles Sir, Gate Mudaliyar, Mudaliyar, and Muhandiram were honorary titles given by the British to the locals during the British rule of Sri Lanka. Those who got those titles were the British government's favorites from high caste rich Sri Lankans. When the British left the country in 1948, they gave a Ranch called Wallauwa to selected people who served them with dedication. One such person was the father of former assassinated Prime Minister Solomon William Ridgeway Dias Bandaranaike. There are many such Wallauwas in many southern villages of the island. They have now become heritage sites and used as locations in Singhala movies."

" It is a piece of interesting information to hear. The name you mentioned is a long name to remember. How did the Sri Lankans remember his long name?"

" Many Sri Lankan Singhalese have long names. The names relate to the village name and their hereditary. The Sri Lankans briefly called him SWRD Bandaranaike. His father was Sir Solomon Dias Bandaranaike, a wealthy man who owned Horogalla Wallauwas. He was a Christian. His roots go to a Tamil Brahmin by the name of Neela Perumal who was a long time back the chief priest of a Pathini temple.

These politicians change religion to become Singhala Buddhist for a political reason to come to power. The last King of Kandy was Tamil Hindu. He changed his religion to Buddhism when he became the King of Kandy by pure luck. He was from the Nayakkar dynasty in South India."

" It is interesting to hear about the roots of the former Singhala Prime Minister. It appears that the name Bandaranayake was derived from Pandaram and Nayaka." Said Watson.

" True Watson and it is a Tamil name linked with South Indian Nayakas "

" Have you ever been to the first Tea estate in Sri Lanka?" Ward asked.

" When I was working as a doctor in Kandy hospital, I have been to the Loolecondera estate which is a hilly and cold village. In Deltota village Sinhalese, Tamils, and Muslims live together. It has a friendly, multicultural environment. Deltota is a remote village, so strangers are easily spotted. I heard that your grandfather James Taylor arrived in1852 in that village. He liked the area at Loolecondera as it had an environment like Scotland. He started the first Tea plantation. The government has constructed a statue for him in that Village. He died in that estate."

"How far is that Tea estate from Kandy?" Mr. Ward asked.

" It is about thirty km from Kandy the hill-country capital. Since the road is winding it will take about an hour and a half by car to reach there."

"What else can I see in Sri Lanka?"

"Interesting places of heritage sites exhibiting the old architecture and history. Sri Lanka's heritage goes back more than three thousand years. beaches, waterfalls, rivers, animal and birds' sanctuaries,

Variety of tropical fruits, Tasty spicy food, and Entertainment. You can also go surfing. Do not fail to visit North and East as it was one of the few Kingdoms that existed on the island," replied Dr. Jeevan.

John Ward said, " I am visiting Sri Lanka to see the tomb of my uncle late Sir John D'Oyly 1st Baronet of Kandy."

"Yes, I have read about him too. He was an excellent colonial administrator during British time and was responsible for drafting the 1815 Kandyan Convention after the Kandyan kingdom was captured by the British and they ruled the entire island. Sir John D'Oyly was in the team that captured the Kandyan King Sri Wickrama Ranasinghe who was hiding in the house The King was deported to Vellore in South India. Sir John D'Oyly died in Kandy and his tomb is in British Amy cemetery in Kandy.

"Thanks, Dr. Jeevan, for the information " replied Ward

"Since both of you are visiting for the first time the island, it is good to know about the 450 years of colonial rule in Ceylon in Sri Lanka before the island got independence in 1948".

" We both love to hear that," said Ward.

" OK, I will tell you briefly about the British system that existed during their rule. My father was working in the government during the British period. I was born a few years before Sri Lanka got the Independence. Before independence, Sri Lanka was under British Madras Presidency, and the currency of Sri Lanka was the Indian Rupees. I started my schooling during the British time, I entered medical college after the independence."

"It is interesting to hear that you started schooling during the British period. So, you would have studied in English, am I right?" Watson said.

" True. English was my major language along with Tamil my mother language. Let me not talk about politics and the dark period created for Tamils after independence. I would say the fault is with the British, because before they left the island. They should have given federal state to North and East just like the way they did for India"

"Yes, I agree with you, but I am sure that the British were misguided by the Majority community leaders of Sri Lanka," replied James.

" I too heard about it. Let me talk about British rule and about that place you would like to see on the island. When I was a doctor, I visited many of those places and in the hill country. There was only one communal riot between Muslims and Sinhalese in 1915 when the British ruled. After the independence, there were many riots and the worst was in 1983 when there was an exodus of Tamils after that riot, Educated Singhalese are good people. I am returning to Sri Lanka after about forty years. I heard stories that the economy of the country is in bad shape. Singhalese is now trying to get out of the country. I know that lot of money is flowing into the country from expatriate Tamils to the families in northern and Eastern provinces and a lot of development work is taking place. I really would like to see personally what these changes are."

" Very good doctor Jeevan. Can you please explain the colonial rule in Sri Lanka?"

" In 1505 Portuguese came as traders to Colombo. They got around the king of Kotte and built a fort. In a few years, they used the family conflict within the King's family to capture the Kotte Kingdom. They took over the cinnamon and spice trade. They chased away the Tamil-speaking Muslim traders from South India called Maraikars. Over time They captured the Jaffna kingdom and coastal areas, but they could not capture the Kandyan kingdom

They built forts in coastal regions and brought east Africans Kaffirs as guards. Portuguese ruled for about 150 years and converted many people to the catholic religion and built many churches. They destroyed Hindu temples and Buddhist Viharas.

After the Portuguese, the Dutch took over and ruled for about one hundred and fifty years. They too could not capture the Kandyan Kingdom. They introduced the Anglican religion and introduced Dutch law and the law called Thesavalami based on Jaffna traditions for Tamils in the Jaffna Kingdom.

After the Dutch, the British took over and captured the Kandy kingdom and ruled the entire island until 1948. When the British gave independence to India in 1947, they thought that it was not worth ruing the small island. Hence, they gave independence to the island called Sri Lanka. The name was changed to Sri Lanka when the island became a Republic. British built administrative systems, roads, rail routes, and schools. They brought Tamil laborers from south India to work in Tea, rubber, coffee, and coconut plantations. They introduced the Police, Postal, and Administrative Civil service. There are old British and Dutch and Portuguese buildings and churches. My father said that Dutch built a Market in my Chunnagam Village, and the Market is a heritage site.

The Portuguese established the city of Jaffna as their colonial administrative center in 1621. Before the army marched into the Portuguese Empire in 1619, the capital of the local kingdom of Jaffna, also known as the Kingdom of the Aryan Emperor,

with Nallur village as the capital.

The Jaffna Fort, built by the Portuguese, was renovated by the Dutch in 1680. From 1590, Portuguese merchants and Catholic missionaries were active within the Kingdom of Jaffna. After 1619, motivated by a permanent fortified settlement, the mercenary forces of the Portuguese army led by Philippe de Oliveira, defeated the last native King, Chnglian II, and captured the Kingdom of Jaffna. Commander de Oliveira moved the political and military control center from Nallur a nearby town of Jaffna, near a fort and harbor.

Portuguese traders took the lucrative trade of elephants from within and claimed the monopoly of elephants from the Vanni area through the port of Columbuthurai, the port of Jaffna, and the importation of goods from Colombo and India. The Portuguese era introduced religious conversion, as well as European education and health care.

In 1658, the Portuguese lost the Kingdom of Jaffna to the Dutch East India Company after a three-month siege. During the Dutch occupation, the city grew in population and size. The Dutch were more tolerant of native trade and religion than the Portuguese. Most of the Hindu temples destroyed by the Portuguese were rebuilt. The community of mixed Eurasian Dutch burgers grew. The Dutch rebuilt the fort and expanded it. They also built Presbyterian churches and government buildings, most of which survived until the 1980s. During the Dutch period, Jaffna gained prominence as a commercial city.

Great Britain occupied Dutch possessions in Ceylon from 1796. Britain maintained many Dutch trades, religion, and taxation policies. During the British colonial period, Jaffna residents' progress in higher education was achieved. All the schools that contributed to the educational advancement of the people of Jaffna were built by missionaries from the American Ceylon Mission, and the Wesleyan Methodist Mission. Under British rule, Jaffna enjoyed a period of rapid growth and prosperity, building major roads and railways connecting the British city with Colombo, Kandy, and other parts of the country. The prosperity of the city's citizens helped them to build temples and schools, as well as a library and a museum.

During the British rule in Sri Lanka. English was the first language. Students learned in English colleges. Tamil or Sinhala was his second language. Arithmetic was also the main subject. Other subjects were History, Geography, etc. Those from affluent families means went to university and graduated. A few sailed for a month by ship via

Suez Canal to England, where they studied and graduated in the bitter cold. Some of the UK-educated rich people on return to the island became ministers and Prime ministers of the country/ A few became prime ministers. Some of them were given honorary titles such as Sir, Gate Mudaliyar, and Mudaliyar. Some who went to study in England did not return as they fell in love with a white woman and were married and settled in England.

People traveled in that period by rickshaw, horse-drawn carriage, or bow-cart. Trolley, Tap Bus, Austin, Morris Minor, Vanguard, cars, and bicycles. There were only a few cinema theaters in Jaffna. There were only a few teachers in Jaffna who have graduated from Sri Lanka. During the British rule, graduate teachers from the states of Tamil Nadu and Kerala worked as teachers in various colleges with a temporary resident visa called TRP's temporary Resident Permit holders.

At that time, the students used a pen dipped for writing on a G Nib pen with ink. Packer pen, swan pen. The Rolex wristwatch was an expensive item. Products made in Japan have no value. The reason is that England was at war with Japan.

Many government servants' salaries were paid on Sterling pounds and the value of a sterling pound was approximately ten rupees. The people had the impression that it was prestige to wear a court suit and tie. But many Tamils and Sinhalese preferred to adhere to their traditional dress. Heads of all government departments were British, and Judges were British." Dr. Jeevan explained the colonial rule of Sri Lanka,

" From what you said it looks that Sri Lankans were happy under the British rule," Watson said.

" Yes, the British gave independence thinking that all communities on the island will live happily, but things went in different directions. Many ethnic riots, rebellions, and corruption, all have affected the economy. I do not know in which direction the island is going." Dr. Jeevan gave his opinion.

****

CHAPTER THREE

A JOURNEY BY YARLDEVI

There was an announcement on Air Lanka that the plane will be landing at Bandaranaike International Airport in half an hour and the passengers are requested to fasten their seat belts, Dr. Jeevan enjoyed the morning breakfast having two hoppers, milk rice, and kattu sambol with milk tea.

He peeped through the window and saw in a cloudless sky the coconut trees and the Negombo lake.

After landing at Bandaranaike International Airport, he saw a much-changed appearance of the Airport building.

From the Aircraft, he took a bus to the terminal with other passengers.

At the immigration when Jeevan handed over the Canadian passport to the Immigration office. He r looked at him and asked,

"Doctor Jeevan welcome to Sri Lanka. When did you migrate to Canada ?"

" Many years ago, after the ethnic riots," he replied to him in the Sinhalese language.

" It appears as if you can still remember to speak in Singhalese language Are you from Jaffna?"

" Of course, I studied in a college in the North and entered medical college. I was working as a doctor in many Sinhalese areas. I had many Singhalese and Muslim friends who studied with me at Colombo medical college."

"How long you are planning to stay in Sri Lanka?"

"Few weeks only."

The officer stamped six months visa and returned the passport to Jeevan.

After passing through the customs, he came out to the arrival terminal

There was a person with a board carrying his name Dr. Jeevan,

Jeevan was happy that Uncle Rajan has arranged for his friend in Colombo to receive him at the Airport.

Dr. Jeevan came out with his baggage and went to the person who was carrying his name board. He introduced himself as Dr. Jeevan.

The man carrying the name board introduced himself as lawyer Alwis. He said to Jeevan that Rajan was a law college friend.

Both got into Alwise's BMW car.

While driving towards Galadhari hotel, Alwis said that his hometown is Moratuwa. After passing his Advance level he entered the law college. He met Rajan at law college Mr. Alwis told him that he visited twice Chunnkam on Rajan's invitation and had Mutton curry, Mangoes, and Palmyra toddy. On the way to the hotel, they stopped and had a King coconut drink.

" Mr. Alwis, I want to take the Morning Express train to KKS tomorrow. Can you please book me a seat?"

" Dr. Jeevan, I have booked a seat for you in an Air-Conditioned compartment on the Yarldevi express train tomorrow morning. It should reach Chunnkam in the afternoon, a journey of about 250 miles. You can have bedfast on the Train. Rajan has arranged for you to stay at Margosa Green lodge in Chunnakam. It is a good hotel with excellent food," replied Alwis.

After reaching the hotel, Dr. Jeevan and Alwis had lunch together at the hotel.

.

"Ok Jeevan you must be tired after a long journey from Toronto. Better have a shower and go to bed. I will meet you a 5.30 AM tomorrow meaning and take you to Colombo Fort Railway Station," Alwis said.

****

The next day while going to the station, Jeevan noticed that many road names have changed to long Singhalese names.

There was a statue of a foreigner in front of the Colombo fort Station. Alwis told Dr. Jeevan that it is the statue of Olcott an American turned Buddhist as such Sri Lankan Buddhists respect him.

****

There were six passengers including Jeevan in the Airconditioned compartment. Most of them were foreign tourists

Jeevan remembered driving to Chunnkam many years ago in his Peugeot 403 car on the Negombo, Puttalam Anuradhapura Vavuniya Kilinochchi Jaffna Road.

At that time, the roads were bad. One day near Omantai he was about to knock his car against a buffalo that was sleeping in the middle of the road on his drive-by car on the A9 highway, he makes it a habit to stop at Murugandy

Ganesh temple, breaks a coconut, burns camphor and continues with his journey. The travelers on that highway believed that unless they stop and break a coconut in that Ganesh temple they may meet with an accident.

Those days it took eight hours by car to reach Chunnkam with a stop for lunch at Anuradhapura rest house.

*****

While on the train the people work in paddy fields and coconut estates. The train stopped at the Rail route junction Ragama. There is a rail route to Puttalam via Negombo and Chilaw along the western coast. After the one-hour journey, hoppers and sambol were served with tea for the breakfast.

The next rail route junction is Polgahawella. The rail route deviates from this junction to the upcountry.

A couple was seated in the opposite seat and introduced themselves as John and Mary from Norway.

"Mr. John, is this your first trip to Jaffna?" Jeevan asked the foreigner.

" Oh no. I visited Jaffna as a representative of the Norway peacekeeping team when LTTE was at war with the Sri Lankan government."

"Did you meet any Jaffna residents?"

" Why not. I met a graduate teacher Manivannan. He could speak English. He served as a translator in our talks with the LTTE team. He said that he lives in Kondavil and invited me to come to his house and have lunch. I could not refuse his invitation. It was excellent food with Jaffna mangoes served for the desert. His wife too was a Tamil teacher."

" What is your opinion about Jaffna people after you meet with Manivannan?"

" I observed that most of the Jaffna people are well educated because there are many Schools in that peninsula built during British, Dutch, and Portuguese rule. Jaffna Tamils are very conservative people and adhere to traditions. The Caste differences existed in many villages. They had their traditions and beliefs. Muslims came to Jaffna as traders from South India. Catholics and Christians live there.

There are many Hindu temples, and, in a few temples, they sacrificed animals. Many residents are farmers involved in tobacco and vegetable cultivation. The soil and water are excellent."

" You are right John. I had education in the English medium in a college in Chunnkam and entered medical college, it was free education ."

" What I heard from Manivannan was that many Tamils youth joined as warriors as they were affected by the educational policy of the government. Some were affected by caste designation."

" Thank God that I was lucky to escape from that policy. So, this is your second visit to Jaffna?"

" Yes, for my wife Mary, it is the first visit. We both will be staying at Manivanna's house at Kondavil. We are going there at his invitation. We will be there for a week sightseeing and enjoying different varieties of mangoes and food."

The train stopped at Anuradhapura a mid-way station

A white color dagoba was visible. Few passengers from the compartment got down at that station.

"Mr. John this town has many heritage sites. It was once called Rajarata which means the city of the kings. Many kings ruled the city. They Ruwnvelisaya Dagoba was started by King Dutugemunu. Even now the politicians talk about him as the Singhala hero who defeated the Chola king Ellara who ruled this city for forty-four years. Buddhism in Sri Lanka started in a village near this city

" I heard that these heritage sites, beaches, and food attract foreign tourists ."

"Tea, Textile, Tourism is the foreign exchange earner for the country," Jeevan said.

The express train reached Jaffna station at noon. Large crows got down in that station.

"John you and your wife will be getting down at two stations next to Jaffna.

I will be getting down at Chunnkam a station after Kondavil. It is pleasure to have met both of you. If both of you come to Canada, please contact me Here is my business card." Jeevan gave his business card to John.

Between Jaffna and Chunnkam there are two stations. The train stops for a few minutes at those stations. In the past both sides of the rail route there were vegetable and Tobacco cultivation and a few roofed houses. But now after many years, the scene has changed. Only a few Tobacco cultivations could be seen, there are many roofed houses. Jeevan thought that expatriate Tamil s must be sending money from the western world to their families in the Northern province to build houses. He remembered reading a Tamil article about how the foreign money flowing into the Northern province has changed the way of living moving away from the old culture. Youth have resorted to violence, kidnapping, and raping. He could remember reading about a gang-raping eighteen-year-old schoolchild.

*****

CHAPTER FOUR

MUDALIYAR MURUGESU

Chunnagam is a village on the Jaffna Peninsula in Sri Lanka, about six miles from Jaffna on the road to a northern port called Kankesanthurai, briefly called KKS. Kankesanthurai was an old heritage harbor. The famous and heritage Karthikeya temple called Mavittapuram temple is located a mile down south from KKS.

The name Chunnakam was derived from the Tamil word Chunnam and Gamma which means a village where Limestone is found. But the old name refers to Peacock. In the past Peacocks roamed in the forests in that village and surrounding villages Some temples in Chunnakam still carry the name Mailing. Chunnakam and the surrounding villages such as Manipay, Uduvil, and Mallakam Chankanai were developed by the Dutch during their one-hundred-and-fifty-year rule.

****

One could boldly say that there are no families in Chunnakam and surrounding villages who do not know Mudaliyar Murugesu in Chunnakam. Murugesu's ancestors came to Chunnakam came from Tirunelveli in Tamil Nadu and settled there. Murugesu's father Selvaraj was a Tax collector called Maniakarar during the British rule. Murugesu studied in English medium like his father at Skandvordaya college which was established during British rule.

Murugesu worked as the administrative officer at the

The Government Agents office was called Kachcheri during the British rule. For his excellent dedicated service as a public servant, he was given the honorary title of Mudaliyar. Before Jeevan's father was conferred the title of Mudaliyar.

Before 1948, Governor Percival Auckland Dyke purchased twenty-seven acres of land in Jaffna, using his funds for his residence and gardens. He served as Government Collector for Jaffna and subsequently Government Agent for the Northern Province for 32 years. He was called Rajah of Jaffna, by the people.

****

Jeevan was born in 1939 in Chunnakam to Murugesu and Nallanachiyar.

Jeevan's father would call his wife Naachiyar. Until 1980, a small Sinhalese population from the south lived in Chunnakam, with Indian Tamils, Muslims, and a few Malayalees living there. On the way to Puthur from the Chunnakam junction, one could see fertile land with red soil and freshwater, about half a kilometer from Chunnkam market there is a stone house on a one-acre land with many rooms.

Murugesu was a non-vegetarian but on Fridays, he turns vegetarian. During Mavittapuram and Nallur temple festival period only vegetarian food is served in his house. Jeevan's paternal grandfather Selvaraja built the first stone house in Chunnkam. Later that house was expanded to appear as

Chettinad style houses that contained six bedrooms, two dining rooms, two bathrooms, and a lar. Murugesu had two servants out of which one was a twelve-year boy from Badulla.

Murugesu expanded the land to have a large garden in front and back yards. The locals called the house " Mudaliyar house." The old house built by Murugesu's father was renovated in the style of Chettinad houses in Tamil Nadu. His friend Chinnappa Chettiyar, who had a pawn brokering business in Jaffna Town recommended the plan. Many Businessmen in Jaffna Town were known to Murugesu as he helped them to get a government license to sell certain imported goods like Singer machine, Parker pen, and Raleigh cycle.

Barber Nagalingam. Washerman Annamalai, and Drummer Thurai during funerals were servants of our household. They were called Kudimagankal. The washerman was called Kattadi because he ties the clothes and beat them on the washing stone.

At funeral houses, the drummer Thura plays the drum. Once a month, Annamalai comes to Jeevan's house to collect and wash the dirty clothes. And for the specials that take place at home, Murugesu will also give Dosti and Sari money for serving the family members.

The Barber Nagalingam comes home once a month and gets a haircut for Jeevan and Murugesu, which happens once in two months.

*****

Murugesu is the Trustee of the Murugan temple and Kannagi temple in his village. He did not have a car. He traveled in a cart drawn by two bulls. He had a Raleigh bicycle fitted with a dynamo. He had good English handwriting.

The Government agent of Jaffna under whom he worked appreciated his handwriting.

When the government agent of Jaffna visits villages to see the development work

Murugesu accompanied him to translate Tamil to English.

The GA's official car driver was Stephen Chelliah. He lived in Chundikuli. He could speak English. He was a good car mechanic as well. He maintained the government official's car. With the permission of the government official, he would bring my father in the car and drop him off at our house every day, and Nachiyar would feed him. At Jeevan, request Stephen drives him around the Chunnkam village in the official car. Jeevan was proud to travel in GA's car. Murugesu did not like it because it is a government vehicle as such, he was against using it for private purposes without GA's approval.

One day Governor Percival Auckland asked Duke Murugesu "How many languages do you know, Mr. Murugesu, other than English and Tamil"?

" Sir I know Latin, Singhala, Malayalam,"

The Government Agent gave his Parker pen to Murugesu to knowing different languages. Murugesu took advantage of his close relationship with the government Agent and helped the villages, temples, and schools.

****

CHAPTER FIVE

NALLANAACHIYAR

When traveling on the Yarldevi train to his village, Jeevan thought about the peaceful face a smile of his mother Nallanachiyar. She never punished Jeevan with a cane when he disobeys her orders. As a punishment to him, she never speaks to him for a few hours until Jeevan apologizes to her for disobeying her. Being the only son in the family Jeevan's parents made sure that he had a friendship with upper-class students. Jeevan's maternal grandfather's name was Perampalam. He was a wealthy man as he worked in Malaysia as Surveyor under British rule. Nallanachiyar was his only daughter. One day Jeevan asked his mother,

"Ammah why did my father take you as a bride from Ellalai village near Chunnkam?"

"Son, my father was a Malayan pensioner. He was a Surveyor at Ipoh. During British rule, many Jaffna Tamils migrated to Malaysia to work and earn money. After retirement, they returned to their villages and bought fertile lands, and built houses in the villages such as Urelu, Ellalai, Urumpirai, and Chunnakam. They received a good pension and lived like Zamindars.

Since my father was rich, he gave dowry for your father who had a job in the British government, "Nachiyar explained in response to a question from her son.

"What is dowry mean mother?"

"According to the customary law called Desavalamai, the property was divided into three categories. They are old age, cold, and searching. Muthusamy is the inherited property of the husband. Seetharam is the inherited property of the wife through her mother. The search is the property that the spouses searched for during their married Jeevan. The son of a family inherits the property of the mother, and the son inherits the property of the father. The search is divided equally between the offspring and the offspring. Thus, the inheritance is kept separately from the husband and wife.

When a widow remarries, her bereavement property is distributed to her bisexual children. When a widower remarries, it is necessary to divide his deceased wife's inherited property equally between his wife's daughters, half of his old property, his wife's sons, and half of his wife's children in the search.

Fifty percent of the property sought to be given to the woman at the time of the divorce must be returned to the woman and given to her in search of fifty. If the man has spent on the woman's dowry, the same amount should be paid to the woman.

These privileges were a protection for the woman during the marital Jeevan and the privileges were protection and status for the woman during the marital Jeevan. It can also be considered as a favorable law giving social recognition to the widow and divorced woman in the society of that time; The work they do when giving a woman a nap depends on the salary available. Some parents not only ask for dowry but also donations ".

"Why bride party should donate money to them, mother? "

"If the sisters of the bridegroom are not married the bridegroom gets donations and gives the sisters the dowry."

"Did my dad get a donation"?

"No son. Your father did not insist on dowry. He told my father that he is not interested in dowry and any donations."

Jeevan paused another question." Mother why is that my friends at school ridicule me by calling me the son of a good carrier."

She smiled and said,

" Some villagers do not understand how the phrase has come in use. That phrase in Tamil refers to the color of walls in the well turning saffron in color. Moreover, the names of the villages have an etymology "

Nallanaachiyar was very friendly with the wives of overseer Nadarajah, Village headman, Village council chairperson, and Apothecary.

    ****

CHAPTER SIX

The Family Helpers

The Barber, The Washerman, Coffin carriers, Pandaram (Cook), and the Drummer were families in the Jaffna Peninsula. They were called in Tamil Kudimagankal as they take part in any important ceremonies such as weddings, and puberty functions. ear piercing ceremony for a newborn baby or at the funeral.

Jeevan while traveling to his village by the Yarl Devi express train, remembered all these helpers with whom he had close contacts. He also remembered his parents' giving gifts to them during festive seasons.

Jeevan remembered an incident that happened when he was about fourteen years of age. The barber Nagalingam and the washerman Annamalai quarreled over the ownership of the two bunch of bananas that was hanging at the entrance during his uncle's wedding. It was customary to give each the bunch of bananas that hangs at the entrance of the wedding house. They also get other gifts and food after a wedding. This system was gradually disappearing.

While doing once two months a haircut for Jeevan, the barber Nagalingam narrates interesting stories about the events that happened in the village. He knows the status and caste of many families in the village.

As far as Jeevan knows, his paternal grandfather's barber was Nagalingam's father Muttulingam. Nagalingam was a man with a smile. He showed betel with tobacco. He carried a tin box in his hand that contained the instruments and soap needed for haircuts and shaving. After Muttulingam's death, Nagalingam carried that box whenever he visits houses for haircutting. He trims the mustache of Jeevan's father in the desired shape.

Nagalingam visits Murugesu's house to do hair cutting and starts his business by placing a chair under the tree in the backyard of Jeevan's house. He spreads a white cloth over it. He opens his tin box that contains the instruments required to do his job. He sharpens scissors and the razor. He starts chewing betel with tobacco and chunam. Red-colored betel juice often splashes when he narrates stories. Jeevan's attention was on the story narrated by Nagalingam. When Naachiyar informs her son that the barber will be coming home to give him a haircut, he never likes it is the day, he goes out to play cricket with his friends.

While hair cutting Nagalingam narrates folk tales and proverbs. some proverbs he frequently narrated that were remembered by Jeevan are

"The face is the index of the mind."

"Look before you leap."

" Do not try to hide the pumpkin in a meal?"

'The cat that got burnt by fire burns will never go near the kitchen."

"Like a cat standing on the wall."

"It's like a wolf cried when the sheep got drenched in the rain."

Nagalingam knew about the lovers in the village where they meet and whether the love affair was a success or not. He also knows about the profession and salary of some people and their caste. He would even create and narrate ghost stories that did not happen.

Nagalingam once told Jeevan that his first son did not want to do the family profession. He wanted to study and go to the university and get a degree and get a government job.

He also said that his second son Ramalingam was planning to start a hairdressing salon in Colombo. His father-in-law agreed to provide necessary financial assistance.

When Jeevan was in Canada, he came to know that barber Nagalingam died of mouth cancer. Jeevan remembered Pandaram Vaithilingam who came with his son to cook for Jeevan's uncle's wedding and lived in Alavetty village. Jeevan also remembered Seelan the leader of the drumming group in Chunnkam village who played the drums for the funeral of Jeevan's grandmother.

Jeevan remembered the argument he had with washerman Annamalai for damaging his favorite shirt.

All the memories of his past life came into his mind during his travel to his village. He was not sure whether all these helpers still live in Chunnagam village

****

CHAPTER SEVEN

THE CHUNNAKAM VILLAGE

Jeevan's father Murugesu studied in English medium for the Cambridge examination at Skandvordaya college. He was good at English, Tamil, and Arithmetic.

Residents called him Mudaliyar Murugesu because he joined the civil service during the British period and was an officer. At Chunnagam, the tiled house was built by Jeevan's grandfather Selvaraja in the thirties. It was the first stone house, in Chunnakam. The other tiled houses were that of overseer Nadarajah Apothecary Subramaniam and that of village headman Ponniah.

Jeevan's mother Naachiyar would often proudly say that her husband Murugesu was related to Kumaraswamy Puluvar of Chunnagam

There was a Pawn brokering shop owned by Chellapah Chettiyar. He gave loans to the farmers. The security is Jewelry or the land the farmer owns, the farmers pay back the loan after selling the products.

Jeevan's Tamil teacher often speaks proudly of Kumaraswamy Puluvar who was born in 1854.

He started studying at Mallakam English School. At the age of eight, he started learning Tamil literature and authored many poems.

The main occupation of the residents of Chunnkam is farming. The land was suitable for tobacco cultivation. In addition, they did vegetable cultivation. The framer used a traditional irrigation system called Thula to irrigate their land. his is one of the inventions of our ancestors to make life easier. Thula is a lever system invented to obtain water for agricultural and domestic use. Often a pole made of poovaram (Thespesia populnea)wood is fitted with scales made of coconut or palm wood. This, which was intertwined with Tamil life, has also been forgotten today. However, when you see it in the East today, some memories of the true thrill spread in the mind. Rather, the farming was done by pumping water from a well.

The wells in these agricultural lands are very deep. Two methods were used to pump water from these wells to the farmland, using a lathe and pumping using a formula mechanism.

It took at least four people, one to hold the rope and pour the water when pouring through the scales. The panchamars usually did the work of trampling the scales during that period.

Landlords were tasked with ensuring that this balance of respect on the lands they directly farmed was the compulsory service of the enslaved citizens.

They avoided using artificial manure.

Chunnkam market was the center where they sell the vegetables to the retailers and obtained cash within a week. They also took their produce to market at Sangaani, Jaffna, and Thirunelveli.

Many Valigamam villagers have disputes over the land boundary and sharing water from a common well. These disputes were heard at Malaakam magistrate courts. Advocate Rajan was a popular lawyer in Chunnakam village, His assistants appeared for such land-related cases, and Rajan appeared for criminal and divorce cases. Whenever a couple comes for divorce, as far as possible, he advises them not to go for the device as it will affect the future of the children. He charged fees based on the status of the client. In many cases, he appeared free. The villagers wanted Rajan to contest the parliamentary election. He refused as he hated politics.

There was an Astrologer at Urelu whose predictions were accurate. He had clients from many parts of the Jaffna peninsula. There was also an Ayurvedic physician by the name of Murugupillai, who was well respected by the villagers. He had an herbal garden.

He also treats for fractures. Jeevan remembered him as he cured a fracture in his hand while playing Cricket. Delivery of babies was done at home by a midwife Parvathy.

Many farmers were not used to banking. They kept their money as spot cash at home in boxes. They saved the money through a local Chit fund run by a lady by the name of Sinnamma.

There are two major types of Cheetu. There are two types of Cheetu namely bidding and non-bidding. The informal ace rests on the trust or goodwill of the holder.

In Tamil society, Cheetu is an important method of saving or collecting money. It is a method of mobilizing not only individuals but also businesses first.

There are problems such as cheating on Cheetu or having difficulty paying.

****

CHAPTER EIGHT

ADVOCATE RAJAN

As soon as the train reached Chunnakam station Jeevan noticed that the appearance of the station has changed during the last few decades.

At the time when he was a student, the station was a small building. When he was at, Colombo Medical College, he traveled by steam engine train several times from that station to Colombo. The person who worked as a station master at that time was Ganesalingam. He was known to Jeevan's father. Ganesalingam was from Meesalai.

When Jeevan saw the name board shoeing as Sivapalan, Jeevan thought to himself that unlike in many stations where the station masters' names were Singhalese names, Chunnakam station had one of the few Tamils station masters.

In the past, there were many Tamil Postmasters and Station

masters. But after the Singhala only act, the number gradually got reduced.

Chunnakam station had a completely distinctive look with a flower garden. A person came to him after and asked him

" Are you Dr. Jeevan?"

"Yes, Uncle Rajan. I am Dr. Jeevan, the son of your uncle Mudaliyar Murugesu. I am happy that you still remember me after many years"?

" Good memory is essential for a lawyer. Jeevan your hair is white now. I remember your smiling friendly face. I think you may be over twenty-five when you left Sri Lanka. How old are you now?"

"Sorry Uncle I do not want to tell you, my age. I am always sixteen, "Jeevan laughed.

"It's okay, that humor is still there with you. Does that cold Climate in Canada suit you?"

" At the beginning, I found it difficult to adjust myself. Since I work in a hospital it is OK."

"Do you have children ?"

" Yes uncle, I have a son and a daughter, both are working."

" The lodge where you are going to stay is about a fifteen minutes' drive from here. You will like that lodge. The name is Margosa lodge. It is not too far from the house where you lived with your parents. We will be passing your house before we reach the lodge ", said Rajan.

Jeevan gave the ticket and got out of the station. An old Austin Cambridge car was waiting for him. There were no other cars parked. Although the car was an old model car, it appeared new.

" Your old model car appears as a new car uncle,"

" The old is gold. Now only a few Austin cars are running in Jaffna. Those days we had A40, and Sommerset, Austin Cambridge cars. I am proud to own this car which is more than forty years old. I have a good mechanic at Mallakam. He could repair the engine He has a person to do tinkering work. That mechanic repairs three-wheelers and two-wheelers. "

On the way to the lodge, Jeevan saw a new building next to the Post office.

"What is that building next to the Post office uncle? it looks like a factory."

"Jeevan is a garment factory that was started a few years back by a man who emigrated to France, from Alavetty. Twenty girls are working in that factory. I am the lawyer of that company. They are exporting clothes ."

" I am happy to hear that expatriate Tamils are investing in Northern province giving job opportunities for Tamils."

Before going to the lodge, Jeevan saw his native house on Puthur Road. The roof of the house where he lived was missing. When he saw the condition of the house where he loved he felt sorry. The land where the house was located was covered with bushes. There was only one mature palm tree. The mango, Jack, nelly trees, and coconut trees were all missing. It looked like someone had cut down the trees and the house might have been damaged by a bomb during s Eelam war. One of the two stone pillars at the entrance to the house was missing, and there was only one pillar left. Jeevan was happy to see that it had the name Murugesu Pavan am written on that pillar.

" Uncle, lucky that the house is still there in a damaged condition. "

" Jeevan the well is safe. It looks as if the villagers are using the well to draw water. A single-foot path on your land is the proof. "

"I know my mother used to say many times that well water is like sugarcane and it's true uncle".

"I am sure that you are exhausted after a long journey. I will not advise you to go down and look at the land and the house. There will be snakes under the bushes. After clearing this land and the damaged house, you can comfortably go inside and see your damaged house.

"Uncle, could you please arrange some laborers

to clear the bushes on the land and clean the house. Put up a thorn fence and an entrance gate made of a tin sheet and put up a board saying that no one should go into this land without permission. I would like to see the land and the house after they have cleared it. I will meet the expenses."

" Do not worry Jeevan. I will get it done as soon as possible. You can see your land and the house in good condition before you return to Canada."

"On this visit, I would like to see what changes have taken place in the villages since I left this country forty years ago. I want to meet and talk to people I know during the time I was studying."

After standing silently for a few minutes at the entrance to the house where he lived many years ago, Jeevan got into the car.

On the way to the lodge, he observed three houses, which were once huts, have turned into tiled houses with stone fences. He thought to himself

that a member of that family must be living abroad.

Within ten minutes the car reached the Margosa Green Lodge.

****

CHAPTER NINE

MARGOSA GREEN LODGE

Hotels like Margosa Green Lodge and Thinnai are two lodges located 3 km from Chunnakam Junction to Punnalaikattuvan junction.

Margosa Lodge is an old house remodeled into a lodge. Margosa means neem tree. There is a garden in front of the lodge with neem trees on both sides of the driveway.

There are large gardens behind the lodge giving the appearance of a park. It is an orchard full of many fruit trees. A well is available with a traditional bathing facility to draw water using a bucket and rope was available for tourists who wish to have a bath in the Jaffna traditional way. There were three Raleigh bicycles, and two scooters for tourists who wish to tour the villages.

For those who wish to travel by three-wheelers, the hotel reception arranges that mode of transport from Chunnkam junction. There was a bow cart. When Jeevan saw the cart, it reminded him of the cart owned by his father. That cart owned by his father was drawn by two bulls that were imported from the town

Mayiladuthurai in Tamilnadu. The bow cart travel preferred by foreign

tourists revealed that the tourists wanted a new experience. The old culture has not changed yet.

Margosa Lodge is a renovated bungalow. That bungalow did not exist in the village during Jeevan's school days. There was only one tea shop and a grocery shop. Over the past forty years, hotels like Valampuri, and Thinnai appeared in the village. The Pallaly International Airport is a short distance away from the lodge. Tourists can reach Colombo by air in an hour. What tourists expect most is to see the ancient historical monuments. Tourists enjoy local dishes and having a bath at Keerimalai pond.

Jeevan could not believe that the manager of this lodge is a Sinhalese. The reason is that Tamil teenagers do not want to do such responsible work. To be a hotel manager you need the training in hotel management and to have the ability to serve customers. The manager, Ramesh Silva, previously had the experience of working in a hotel in southern Sri Lanka. Eight out of thirty lodge employees are Sinhalese, and one is Muslim. Others are all Tamils.

The main chef in this lodge is a Tamil. A Sinhalese helps him in cooking. In the lodge, a music group sings songs The type of food with Jaffna songs reflects the Jaffna culture. The Goat, Chicken. Fish curries. And vegetables are present in all types of food. Fruits were mangoes, bananas, papayas, guavas. There was a separate room for Jeevan with a Refrigerator and TV the room.

The manager told Jeevan, "Doctor, you can take a bath in the well if you want."

Jeevan knew from the way the manager called him Doctor, that Rajan Uncle would have

briefed about Jeevan that he was born in that village.

" Mr. Rajan told me that your parents were famous men in this village. So, I need to brief you about this village. You have come to this village many years after migrating to Canada with memories of the village where you studied and grew up."\

" True, I love to see the changes."

"Where was your house?"

"My native house is not too far from this lodge . It is about a kilometer away and now that house is in ruins. I have come to sort out things ".

"Mr. Rajan told me that you were a doctor and you studied in Colombo,"

"Yes, Ramesh I studied at Colombo Medical College and became a

doctor. I worked in Sinhalese towns. I migrated to Canada after the 1983 riots."

"I know t another Tamil man who was a doctor and he emigrated from Trincomalee. He was politically victimized ."

Many Tamil doctors migrated after the ethnic riots,"
****

Jeevan decided to go cycling. He had good memories of riding a hired bicycle around the village during his school

days. Then his father bought him a rally bicycle. Jeevan will go to school on that bicycle. Ravi used to go to Jaffna with his friends sometimes. Ravi's younger sister Rathi is a Rathi Devi model, with attractive eyes,

Long hair. Her laughter then came to Jeevan. Overseas Nataraja family are close acquaintances with the Jeevan family. Jeevan with us often goes overseas home. Overseer Nadarajah's wife Kanagamma was Jeevan's mother's close friend. Both participated in the Chit fund organized by Chinnamma.

"My daughter Rathy looks incredibly happy when she sees your son Jeevan in this house. They both are a good match. "

Jeevan's mother never commented on what Rathy; s mother said.

***

Jeevan opened the windows of his room at Marcosa Lodge and breathed in the fresh air. The hotel employee came and knocked on the room door.

"Let's come in."

"Do you want to drink anything?" The visitor asked.

"What do you have to drink?".

"I can bring fresh fruit juice".

"Can I have papaya juice?"

" No problem, Sir. I will bring it." Jeevan knows that many kinds of fruit are available in Chunnkam.

'Can I have a Karutha Colomban mango?"

" I will bring it sliced. It is a fresh one."

In a few minutes, the waiter brought the items Jeevan ordered.

Jeevan asked the waiter where the Mango came from.

" The lodge received the mangoes from Meesalai village ."

Jeevan slept for two hours. He got up and had a shower and got ready to go out.

****

First Jeevan decided to go to the nearby Kannaki Amman temple and see how the temple in a bicycle.

He cycled twice in Canada. But he does not know what the roads are like here. He took his bicycle and started the journey exploring the town.

****

He never sighted anyone on the road. He saw only a few shops. One was a bicycle shop, a tea shop, and the other a grocery store,

The Kannaki Amman Temple is located on a ten-foot-wide tarred road that runs west towards Punnalaikattuvan. Gardens on both sides but now we will see how it is Kannaki Amman went towards the temple. While cycling to Kannagi temple he saw a bus bearing the nameplate Alavetty.

Jeevan saw a cart loaded with coconut husks. It brought back old memories to Jeevan. He was glad that these bat carts still existed in the village.

*****

CHAPTER TEN

THE KANNAKI TEMPLE

Many years ago, a Kannaki Amman temple existed in a small hut on the Puthur road not too far from Margosa lodge. Jeevan's father collected money and with his contribution expanded the temple. Many tears ago there was a narrow gravel lane to the Temple from the Chunnkam Puthur road. A car could not go in that lane.

There were vegetable gardens on both sides of the lane. He feared the stray dogs. Jeevan remembered walking on that lane with his parents to attend a Pongal festival in that temple. The villagers believed that the power of Kannaki in that temple protected the villagers from infectious diseases.

Jeevan went by bicycle that was available to the temple. He was happy to note that the lane to the temple has developed into a fifteen-foot wide-tared road.

Houses appeared in the vegetable gardens that were there many years ago. The appearance e of the temple has changed. It appeared as a temple with gopuram. There were stone walls around the temple painted in Red and white stripes symbolizing that it is a Hindu temple. He saw that the temple had a bell tower. Next to the temple was a wedding hall.

This temple has a history. There is no record of when this temple appeared in that location. Jeevan's father once told him that a farmer who had farming land while cultivating found a Kannagi statue in a well on that land.

The idol that was found by the farmer was placed in the hut and worshiped by him and the people living in that area

.

He also told him that Kannagi Amman worships as Pathini worship in Sri Lanka back to the second century AD. King Gajabahu who ruled at that period brought back his lost 12,000 men from India and

also brought the idol of Goddess Pathini after attending a festival for Kannagi in Kerala organized by King Seran Senkutuvan who was ruling the Kerala Kingdom. Serna's brother authored the story of Kannagi as Silapathikaram

Gajabahu pm his way to his palace in Anuradhapura from Maathgal a port in Jaffna and establish several temples for Pathini. It may be that there was a temple for Kannagi in that area. During the Portuguese rule of the Jaffna kingdom, they were destroying many Hindu temples. To protect the Kannagi idol, the worshippers would have dropped the idol into the well in the farmland. After many years, the farmer found the Kannagi statue from the well and established a temple in a hut.

There is a small wedding hall in the temple that was generating revenue for the temple through weddings and other functions in addition to the money paid by worshippers.

Jeevan remembered attending a Pongal festival in that temple. On the Pongal festival day, they narrated the story of Kannagi.

****

When the temple priest saw Jeevan, he looked at him and asked him, "Aiyah, I have not seen you before coming to this temple. Are you new to this village ?"

Jeevan said, " I am an old resident of this village. I was away from the village for many years. That is why you are not able to identify me. "

He laughed and asked, " If so, whose son, are you?"

"I am Dr Jeevan the son of Mudaliyar Murugesu and Nallanachiyar. He was a well-known person to the villagers.

My father helped in changing the temple from a hut to a temple in a stone building."

Once the priest came to know that he was talking to the doctor, .son of Mudaliyar Murugesu, his tone changed.

" I am sorry doctor I could not recognize you. I did not know you are Mudaliyar Murugesu's son. My father who was the priest of this temple died many years ago, praised your father. He also once told me that your father had a son who qualified as a doctor and migrated to Canada. I am glad to meet you after many years. This temple is supported by many people from this area who migrated to many countries after the war."

" I am glad to hear that," Jeevan said

" Now that you have come to this temple can I do puja for you and your family "

"Why not Aiyar?

"What is your star?" He asked.

"Please do the puja in the name of my family."

He went inside the temple and chanted the mantra in Sanskrit in front of the idol of Kannagi for half an hour and came out with puja items on a plate. The priest gave Jeevan holy ash and Kunkumam.

Jeevan gave one thousand rupees on the plate.

It was a surprise for the priest to receive that large amount of money

"Thank you so much Dr. Aiyah for giving me so much money on the spot".

"Does this temple need any other help" ?.

He thought for a moment and said, "Yes Doctor, this temple needs some lanterns and some utensils to cook and serve the poor."

"How many times do you give alms".

"Twice a month we give alms. At the same time, some villagers come and give alms."

" For how long the festival happens?" Jeevan asked

"It is a one-week festival including a Pongal festival but there is no

chariot festival ."

"What are the other activities in the temple?"

"Kannaki Amman story songs are narrated
once a month."

"I am giving you twenty thousand rupees to buy brass lamps and utensils". Jeevan gave him cash

A receipt was given by the priest

"Thank you, doctor, for donating money to the temple," Iyer said.

"My lawyer Rajan will come in a few months to see if you bought the items ."

The priest served Dr. Jeevan milk rice and fruits.

After speaking to the priest, Jeeva left the temple on the bicycle

****

CHAPTER ELEVEN

THE FAMER VEERAVAGU

Jeevan on his way to meet Rajan at the entrance to the cemetery decided to visit the Bairava temple located on farmland. He remembered that temple, as goats were sacrificed at the temple once a year. He once saw that animal sacrificing festival and got sick of it.

When Jeevan came to the main road, he saw a cart that was carrying Kiduku. He spoke to the man who was driving the cart,

" Aiyah from where you are bringing these Kiduku ?"

" Brother Coconut leaves are used in roofing and fencing. Although the coconut husk is exceptionally large, it cannot be used for roofing or fencing as it is in compact areas on either side of a stalk. But by knitting, they become large enough to be flat enough to be used for fencing and roofing. This we call Kiduku in Tamil. We bring this from Palai, an area where there are many coconut estates."

"I know that Palai is a village far away from Chunnkam on the Jaffna Kandy Road. When did you start this cart journey?"

" Yesterday, Aiyah, my son accompanies me. There is a good demand for Kiduku in Valigamam. On our return journey, we take leaves cut from the trees in fences and sell as natural manure for cultivation in the Thenmartachi area ."

Jeevan was incredibly happy to hear that the old method of traditional fencing is used in some villages.

Jeevan saw a bus half-full of passengers traveling towards Chunnagam junction The Board on the bus showed as Alavetty. The appearance of the bus has changed.

Many years ago, the bus was in the shape of a box. People called it Thattu box.

When Jeevan reached the Bairva temple he noticed that Temple too had changed in its appearance. Jeevan asked a farmer who was there cleaning the temple.

"Aiyah are you in charge of this Bairva Temple ?"

" Yes, l look after the temple from the time this temple is located on my land, I am Veeravagu, the owner of this land."

" Do people still sacrifice goats and fowls to this Bairava "?

He looked at Jeevan and asked "Aiyah are you new to this town?

"No, Aiyah. I am from this village. My native house is on this road."

"Oh, I see. Whose son, are you?

" I am Dr. Jeevan's son of late Mudaliyar Murugesu I emigrated to Canada. I did not come to this village where I was born for more than 40 years. I came to see what changes are taking place in this village."

" Oh god. I know your father well. He helped many people. I am glad to hear that you are the son of Mudaliyar Murugesu. In Chunnakam everything has changed. My name is Veeravagu. I am a farmer."

" I see. You did not answer the question I asked, before"?

"Yes Aiyah, people do not Sacrifice goats now. The youth association in Chunnkam is against animal sacrifice. They filed a case against animal sacrifice

and won."

" That is good Veeravagu In the name of God, we were violating animal rights."

"Aiyah after stopping that sacrifice the yield in here is very low".

"Aiyah that's not the reason, it is because you have to cultivate using new farming methods. Use good natural fertilizers. Do not use chemical fertilizers. Only then will the crops be good."

"What you are saying is not only true, Aiyah. Now that the number of people who smoke cigars has decreased, there is not much demand for tobacco. Doctors say smoking can lead to heart disease and cancer, so many framers stopped cultivating tobacco. I too have stopped cultivating it.

"I'm a doctor, and I know that smoking is not only bad for the heart, but it can also cause cancer. It is better to avoid cultivating tobacco."

The farmer said, "The victims are farmers and cigar workers. Once upon a time in Jaffna, Kanaglingam cigars, cigars had excellent value. "

"I do not know whether in a few more years there will be any gardens around this area"

"What you say is true Dr. Aiyah", Veeravagu replied.

After talking to him Jeevan went towards Chunnakam junction.

Before going to the junction, he wanted to see the cemetery where his father and mother were cremated. He also wanted to see the neem tree in the cemetery where he and his friend Ravi engraved on the bark of the tree their names and his friend Ravi's sister Rathydevi's names.

Jeevan was eager to see if those names existed in the bark of the neem tree.

At the entrance to the cemetery, Rajan was waiting in his car to meet Jeevan.

Rajan was surprised to see Jeevan riding a bicycle

" Jeevan, it looks like you are enjoying cycling in this village,"

" Of course, uncle. It reminds me of my memories during my school days. Let us keep the bicycle in the car boot and walk to the cemetery. I want to see the place where my parents have cremated and the Neem tree, where I engraved names."

" Why not Jeevan. I see a corpse burning and the cemetery keeper is busy burning it."

****

CHAPTER TWELVE

THE VILLAGE CEMETERY

A group of villages in Valigamam North has a common cemetery where cremations are done as per Hindu rites. There are also burial places

for other religious people. The cemetery is located two kilometers to the south

of Chunnkam Market on the road to Puthur. It is maintained by the local town council. There is a person who does the cremation or burial.

The cemetery is located about half a kilometer from Mudaliyar Murugesu's house on Chunnakam Puthur road. Muthan is the cemetery keeper. He took over the job from his father Kandan after his father died at the age of eighty. Muthan was helping the father to cremate the corpses. The relation of the dead person pays for all expenses such as Firewood, rituals, and cremation.

Both walked towards the cemetery. At a distance, a corpse was burning.

"Uncle Rajan, a long time back the cemetery was surrounded by thorny bush. There was a neem tree near the hut in the cemetery where ceremonies are held for the corpse before cremation. I could see that tree still there"

" Jeevan what brought you to see the cemetery? Rajan asked.

"Uncle I want to speak to Muthan who cremated my parents. I could not come to the village to do the rituals for my parents. It was my duty. I regret it. I also want to see the neem tree where I and my friend Ravi engraved our names. I engraved Ravi's sister Rathy's

name as well:"

" So, Jeevan you still remember Overseer Nadarajah; 's son Ravi and daughter Rathy ."

" Of course, uncle. How can I forget them? Ravi's parents

were our family friends. I want to meet both."

" I am sorry Jeevan you cannot meet Ravi. After you left for Canada, he was

frustrated that he could not enter the University. So, he decided to join the Tamil Tiger, liberation movement. He fought and died as a hero at the Elephant Pass battle with the government forces."

" I am sorry to hear that news uncle. When he was a student, he had

links with that group. I advised him to concentrate on his studies. He had a different view. How about his sister Rathydevi? Is she in Chunnakam? Is she married? I like to meet her ."

" Jeevan, Ravi's sister Rathy is not married. She is living still as Ms. Rathydevi Nadarajah. After you left the island, she was

upset and refused to entertain any marriage proposals for her. Her parents knew that she had a soft corner for you. But she was very unfortunate that she could

noy marry you."

" Uncle it is fate that decides the marriage. Where is she now?"

" She was teaching at Uduvil girls' college. After retirement, she is now working as a manager of a senior's home at Uduvil."

" Uncle I want to meet her. Can you please take me to that senior's home ?"

" Why not. I have her name in my list of people whom you wish to meet."

Jeevan and

Rajan walked towards the Neem tree. The hut that was there is now replaced by a small hall with a platform to keep the corpse and do rituals.

Jeevan inspected the three names engraved by him and Ravi in the bark of the tree. The bark of the neem tree has grown thicker. After reading and photographing the names, Jeevan e stayed there for a few seconds and recollected the day the names were engraved.

It was a Saturday. During the weekend he and Ravi visit Jeevan's Raleigh bicycle villages, temples, and heritage locations. Jeevan and Ravi decided to watch how a body is cremated in the cemetery. After watching the burning of a corpse, they both decided to engrave their names on the bark of the Neem tree. Ravi used the penknife he had with him. He gave it to Jeevan to engrave his name first, after him, Ravi engraved his name. After engraving both names, Jeevan remembered Rathy. He had a soft corner for her. Whenever Jeevan drops Ravi in his Raleigh cycle at overseer Nadarajah's house after school, Rathy made use of that opportunity to talk to him by inviting him to come to the house to clear some doubts related to Botany and Chemistry subjects. Ravi too encouraged their friendship.

After engraving and dating the two names Jeevan said "Ravi, we both have forgotten to engrave your sister Rathy's name. With your permission can I please engrave it ."

Ravi smiled and said "Why not. I know that You like her. So, she too."

After recollecting that incident Jeevan said to Rajan " Uncle these names were engraved more than four decades years ago. Look at the date. It proves

how our friendship was ."

"Jeevan, I value your friendship. It is a pity that the friendship did not continue."

Muthan who was burning the corpse saw Rajan and came and met them. It was Muthan who cremated Rajan's parents

" Aiyah who is this person who is with you?" Mutaiyan asked Rajan.

" What Muthan cannot you identify him. He is Mudaliyar

Murugesu Aliyah's son Doctor Jeevan. I am sure you knew him as a

student ."

" Oh my god. What a change in him. I am seeing him after many years. He was a handsome young man. I knew that he was away from this country. He did not come to do rituals for his parents when he died. I who burnt their bodies. Mudaliyar Murugesu Aiyah and his wife were great people. Whenever he saw me, he inquired about my family and gave me money. For the Pongal, he gave me clothes and money."

Jeevan apologized to Muthan giving the reason as to why he could not attend his parents' funeral. He inquired about his son Seelan. Muthan told him that his son died at the army attack at the Chunnkam market.

Jeevan gave him two thousand rupees for the services he is rendering.

"Uncle I remember the ghost stories associated with the cemetery.

"What are the stories you are talking about Jeevan?" Rajan asked.

"Uncle I could remember the two accidents at the entrance to this cemetery in which two died in two car accidents. People were scared to pass this cemetery.

There was gossip in the village that if anyone crosses the entrance to this cemetery, they will see a ghost of a woman in a white saree with long hair.

Some said it was a Mohini devil. Still, others said that if a woman who had a love failure and committed suicide, she is looking for her boyfriend."

" Jeevan Aiyah, as you said these stories are all gossip. I never saw any woman in a white dress. I cremate corpses in the middle of the night. To keep me active I normally take a half bottle of arrack. At times, my sister's husband helps me with the cremation. The relations of the dead people whose bodies are created give me money and a bottle of arrack ."

"Muthan it is a pleasure to meet you after

many years. Continue doing this good service. Rajan's uncle and I must meet many people. We both must

go now "

*****

Both came out of the cemetery. Jeevan pointed out to Rajan a farming land next to the cemetery and said'

" Uncle my maternal uncle Balan once owned two-acre land. He participated in vegetable cultivation. On weekend I helped him to water the plants and in plucking vegetables. There was a leaver system called "Thula." I used to walk up and down on the lever to make it easy for my uncle Balan to

draw water. He is to pay money for the help I provided. Ravi and I spent that money by seeing Tamil movies at the wellington movie theater at Jaffna. We both go there on my bicycle. Now I do not see that Thula"

" Jeevan, now farmers do not use the old Thula system to water the plants. They have switched on to water pumps. It is faster and does not require much labor."

" Uncle I see a factory building in a section of the land. What is that building?"

"Jeevan, your uncle sold his land to an expatriate Tamil called Manoharan

living in Australia. It was I who did that land transfer He started a water bottling factory. You know very well there is excellent quality water in this area. A long time back you are aware that water in wooden barrels is sent from Chunnakam station to Colombo by train. Now you will not see those water barrels at the Railway station. Things are changing with time. Everything is business-related to generate money. Now you get water in plastic bottles. There is a factory that bottles water and sends them to Colombo ."

" You are right uncle. Water in a plastic bottle was given on the train. I also saw the carts coming from Chavakachcheri with coconut husks and Kiduku. They sell them here and crop the leaves from the trees in the fences and take them back and sell them as manure to framers, Now I do not see those carts."

"Now farmers hardly use natural manure. They use imported inorganic manure. The method of farming has changed Jeevan."

" Uncle I noticed that old fences with trees on them have disappeared. In that place, stone walls have come up."

"True Jeevan expatriate Tamil people's money has changed the old traditional fences to the stone fences. They say it provides security to the land Moreover no recurring cost is invited in replacing the fence once in a few years. But I do not wish to replace the fence in my house with brick walls "

" Why uncle. You can afford to replace the fence with a stone fence."

" Jeevan you would have seen from my old Austin Cambridge

car. I did not go for the new Japanese cars. In the same way, I want the trees in the

fence to stay there. I love nature. In addition, it helps farmers with natural manure and helps some people who travel from Chavakachcheri to earn a living."

"Uncle your policy is great. I appreciate it. Not everyone thinks the way you think. Few people only stick to the old traditions," Jeevan said.

*****

CHAPTER THIRTEEN

THE CHUNNAKAM MARKET

Three centuries ago, During the Dutch and British periods, the rulers encouraged the farmers to do more farming and sell their products in a Marketplace. The rulers-built markets in many places in Jaffna Peninsula. To name them the main market in Jaffna town, markets at Kodikaamam, Chavakachcheri , Chankanai, Thirunelveli , Kalviyan Kadu and Chunnakam . The rulers collected Taxes from the shops in the market.

Out of these markets, the popular market is the Chunnkam market. The market was built by the Dutch during the 18th century. The building is still there, symbolizing that colonial architecture.

The Dutch selected Chunnkam village to build the market as it is located at the central spot in the farming villages and on the road to KKS.

Moreover, there is a railway station located not too far from the location of the market.

Chunnkam market building plays the same role as a heritage building today. It was built over three hundred years ago. Chunnakam market is a thriving marketplace serving the town from vegetables to clothes and mobile phones. Different items are sold at the various shops in the market.

Unfortunately, new sheds have been set up to open room for new hawkers covering this magnificent building from all sides. Although declared as an archaeological monument, the central Dutch building is badly in need of maintenance if not conservation.

Chunnakam Junction is the junction of Kandarodai on the west, Puthur via Punnalaikattuvan on the east, and the road from Jaffna to Kankesanthurai. There is a Chunnakam market near this junction. There are Textile, Computer, Fruit juice, Bookstall, Aluminum vessels, Fish, Dry Fish, Meat, Tailoring, Aluminum utensils, Cigar, Grocery shops. An ayurvedic doctor had an herbal shop.

There was a takeout Dosai shop run by a lady

by the name of Visalatchi. The fish and

meat shops are in a separate section. There are many vegetable and fruit shops. People come from adjoining villages to buy things, In the past,

there was only a Bus stop opposite the Market.

It was one of the major markets in the Jaffna Peninsula.

****

Jeevan and Rajan left the cemetery to the Chunnkam market. Jeevan was interested in exploring the changes in the market over the last forty or more years. He also wanted to meet some shopkeepers known to him during his school days. He remembered visiting the shop with his mother and the servant boy to buy things. In particular, he remembered the Book shop where he bought Tamil

Magazines that were imported from South India. The Book shop also sold schoolbooks and newspapers, as well as literary Tamil books written by writers from Sri Lanka.

He liked the hoppers and Dosai sold at Visalatchi's shop. Jeevan was very friendly with the lady as she serves food in a receptacle made from palmyra leaf and at times on banana leaf, Jeevan; s dress was stitched by Maulanas tailoring shop. He sold

lungees imported from south India. Maulana's son Baseer worked as the cutter in the tailoring shop.

Another shop he remembered was Thurai's pottery and receptacle shop. He was

related to his father Murugesu. He remembered his father helping him to establish the shop.

After visiting vegetables and groceries. Textile shops Jeevan remembered his mother taking him to buy fish from fishmonger Anthony Pillai from Sillalai. Anthony started Jeevan as a fisher at Mailiddy and later became a fishmonger. He gets fresh fish from various fishing villages.

Jeevan liked cuttlefish, prawns, crabs, and Kingfish. Jeevan's mother never bought mutton from the meat stall, as she was of the view that the goat meat sold was not good

. Goat Meat was supplied directly to their home by a Markandu alias Mark once a week slaughters two goats and sells the meat to houses that placed the orders in advance Mark's son does the delivery service. Markandu also sold goat liver and heart, the goat brain, intestines, and blood, to those people who order them in advance.

Mark was the main slaughterer of goats at the annual slaughtering of goat festival at Biravar temple. One day without getting permission from his parents Jeevan attended the festival with his friend Ravi.

That was the first and last day he went to the festival. Since he was watching the chopping of the goat's head by Mark in one chop, the blood splashed on his shirt. He returned home and was punished by his mother for attending the goat cutting festival.

****

While driving in Rajan's car from the cemetery to the Market he rendered his experience in visiting the market as a student with his mother

Jeevan saw a new building for the Post office and the Police station. The Chunnakam Railway station has a new building with seating arrangements and a garden. When Jeevan was at Colombo medical college, he frequently traveled by train drawn by a steam engine. His father ensured that his son traveled comfortably in the first-class compartment. Only a few people traveled by first class. The train from KKS to Colombo fort station, a journey of about 250 miles stopped at several stations and took more than ten hours. Jeevan's mother prepared and gave him a lunch packet with a thermos flask full of coffee to be taken on the train.

*****

CHAPTER FOURTEEN

THE UTENSILS SHOP OWNER THURAI

Rajan dropped Jeevan at the market and went to his office located not too far from the Market. When Jeevan walked into the Chunnkam market he saw everyone staring at him. One inquisitive man in the market asked Jeevan whether he is new to the market so that he can take him around and show him the market as a tourist guide.

"Do not worry. I need no guide. I was born in Chunnagam. I have been to this market several times." He walked ignoring the man.

Jeevan remembered the Pottery and aluminum receptacles shop owned by Thuraisingam. He is a relation of Jeevan's mother. Jeevan's mother called him Thurai. Jeevan called him Thurai's uncle.

Jeevan met Pottery shop owner Thurai. At old age, he had a beard and was actively selling utensils to customers. Jeevan could not see Thura's son Vasanthan who studied at Skandvordaya college.

" Thurai Uncle can you remember me, " Jeevan asked Thurai.

Thurai stood speechless for a few seconds and then said, "My god you are Mudaliyar Murugesu's son Jeevan. Am I right?"

" Yes, uncle. I am Jeevan. A long time back you saw me as a boy. It is great that you identified me after many years."

" How can I forget your parents who helped me financially to start this shop. You visited my shop as a boy with your mother. I gave a till box in the shape of a pig as a gift to you."

" Yes, uncle. I remember that beautiful till box. I have that with me in Canada. I told my family the sentimental value of that till box."

" I am glad to hear that, Jeevan. Those are the golden days when everyone in this village and market knows each person. I heard from my wife that after becoming a doctor you migrated to Canada many years ago ."

Jeevan explained to Thurai the reason he migrated and apologized to him why could not come to his parent's funeral.

"Uncle where is your son Vasanthan? He studied at Skanda. He was a year junior to me. He was in the school cricket team."

" Jeevan please do not remind me of the incident where my son was killed by the army when they attacked this Market. At that time, I was not in the shop. He was looking after the shop. The army never liked Tamil youth. He was one of their targets."

Jeevan was shocked to hear Vasanthan got killed during the Army's attack on the market.

At the request of Jeevan Thurai narrated the attack by the army.

" Thamby Jeevan since you are asking for the details of the attack. On 28 March 1984, personnel belonging to the Sri Lankan military arrived at the market in tanks and jeeps and opened fire for no reason at the crowd in both these places. Eight civilians were shot dead, and over fifty were injured. My son was one of the people who were killed. Tailor Maulana's son too got killed. Visalatchi was lucky. On that day she was sick and did not open her Dosai shop. The military then proceeded to set fire to the market and burnt down all the shops contained within it.

The military then left the location and drove through Mallakam and Tellipalali along the Kankesanthurai road. There, they started shooting at everyone, who came within their sight. One civilian was killed, and female students in Tellipalali, who were returning home from school after completing their examinations were assaulted. Consequently, twenty-six students were injured. And another than twenty civilians belonging to these two villages were also injured."

" Uncle I faced the same situation in Colombo during riots by Singhalese mobs instigated by the government. That was why I migrated to Canada. I am working as a doctor there. I am married to a Malaysian Tamil I have a son and daughter."

" I am happy to hear that you are married to a Tamil woman and have two children. What made you visit Chunnkam after many years?"

Jeevan explained to him the reason for his visit to Chunnkam.

Thurai told him that he rebuilt his business by taking a bank loan, He did not get any compensation from the government for the attack by the army. He is yet to pay about twenty thousand rupees to the bank.

After hearing about Thurai's financial problem, he promised him that he will decide with lawyer Rajan to settle his Bank loan.

Thurai never expected that Jeevan will settle his Bank loan. Tears appeared in his eyes. He held Jeevan's hands, kissed and thanked him.

He said to him Jeevan "Thamby Jeevan, you are just like your father who was a great philanthropist. He helped many people to start the business."

Jeevan inquired about their father's relation with Maniam who collected protection money from the shop owners in the Market. Thurai told him the story of how Maniam was killed by a student. He also explained to him that, the temple dancer Chinthamani, Maniyam's lover is now living in poverty with her daughter through her love affair with Maniam.

Jeevan obtained the addresses of Visalatchi and Chinthamani from Thurai as he was keen to meet them and help them.

Jeevan inquired about fishmonger Anthony from whom his mother bought fish.

Thurai said " Thamby Jeevan Anthony who was a smoker died of lung cancer a few years back, His son is running a shop in the fish market. As you knew him you can meet him in the fish market. He is the only man with a bald head man among the fish sellers."

Jeevan thanked Thurai and left for the fish market to meet Anton's son Soosai. He saw the fish mongers calling customers by mentioning different varieties of fish.

****

The fishmonger Anthony was known to Jeevan in the market when he was a student, Jeevan knew Anthony's son Soosai as well. Anthony participated in fishing at

Mullaitivu. He moved out from Mullaitivu as fishermen from the south started fishing in Mullaitivu. The army did not allow the fishers to fish there either, as the area was under military occupation. Anthony stopped fishing and returned to his hometown of Uduvil. He started to sell fish in the Chunnkam market. As he was a fisherman he knew about different verities of fish.

Jeevan went to the side where the fish mongers are. He saw people bargaining for a cheaper price. There were two ladies seated in the corner cleaning the fish bought by customers. Jeevan remembered his mother getting the fish cleaned by a lady Ponni, before taking it home. Jeevan inquired from the ladies who were cleaning the fish about Ponni. She pointed out a young lady who was claiming fish and said "Aiyah, Ponni died a long few years ago. That young lady who is cleaning the fish is Ponni's daughter Thnagam."

None of the faces in the fish market were familiar to him. When Jeevan saw the bald heeded man Soosai, he went to him.

"Aiyah, I have fresh fish. Do you want any fish?" Soosai asked.

"Soosai, I am Jeevan, Mudaliyar Murugesu's son I know you as a young man and your father Anthony. Are you Anthony's son?

"Oh yes, now I remember you. My father, before he died told me about how your father Mudaliyar Murugesu helped him to start selling fish in this market and you liked King fish and Crabs. Your father and mother advised him to stop smoking. My father could not stop smoking. That caused him his death. I have taken over his shop and run it. There is heavy competition. Moreover, the fishers sell the best fish they catch at a high price to hotels. We cannot compete with hotels."

"Do you smoke Soosai?"

" No Jeevan Aiyah, I am thinking of joining my friend from Myliddy to go out in the sea and do fishing, He has a motorboat."

" How is your mother, Mary. My mother liked her as she taught my mother how to knit."

" She is old and bedridden. My younger brother Jesu who was a car mechanic went to Australia by a cargo ship. He is now an Australian citizen and has a car repair shop there. He sends money to look after my mother. Why not you see my mother. She speaks extremely high of your parents ."

" Soosai if I have time, I will visit your mother. I know your house. Keep these two thousand rupees with you. This money may help you in your business and buy medicine for your mother."

" Thank you, Jeevan Aiyah, please keep this small conge in remembrance of me." Soosai gave a white conge to Jeevan.

From the market, Jeevan walked towards the shops in the town and explore the changes.

****

CHAPTER FIFTEEN

THE CHUNNAGAM TOWN SHOPKEEPERS

When Jeevan was a student, he remembered a few shops and a restaurant called Ananda Bhavan at that junction. A clothing store, a grocery store.

Bicycle repair and rental shop. During that period, the cycle repairer charged Ten cents to blow two tires per bicycle. Bicycle rent is fifty cents per hour. Cars were a rarity at the time. Few Austin A40 cars are often seen on the Jaffna-KKS Road. Skandvordaya college is located 2.5 km North of the junction on the way to Alavetty. During school days gave a lift on his Raleigh bicycle fitted with dynamo and light to his favorite friends. Ravi, the son of Overseer Nadarajah, often gets a

lift from school on Jeevan's bicycle. Rathy Devi, the pretty younger sister of Ravi gets a chance to meet and talk to Jeevan and clear her doubts about science subjects. She normally does not talk to everyone. She is proud of her beauty, but when she sees Jeevan, she welcomes him with a smile.

There were two grocery stores at Chunnagam Junction, one of which belonged to Ismail Nana and the other was the Murugan shop. Illicit liquor is available only to those who personally know the owner of the Murugan shop.

Jeevan went to the shop where Ismail Nanna's shop was, But the shop has

changed hands and the shop name was changed to Lucky

Stores. The owner was Eswaran.

" Aiyah, do you know where the

former owner Ismail of this Shop is?" Jeevan asked the new owner.

The owner of the shop replied, "Are you new to this town?"

" Oh no. I was born in the village of Chunnakam. I was away from this

village for many years."

" I see, well when the Tamil tigers suspected the Muslim community as informers to IPKF force, they ordered all Muslims on the Jaffna peninsula to leave Northern province within a few hours.

Ismail did not have any other option; he sold the shop at an extremely low price and went to Puttalam I heard that he has a grocery shop there

There was the Valigamam communist party office. Many workers who were members came to that office to get advice when they have issues with the employer,

A politician by the name, of Ponnampalam from Alavetty, was a member of the Ceylon Communist Party that was continually active in that period.

In the sixties, there was a Mavittapuram Kandasamy Kōvil temple entry issue. Low caste people were not permitted to enter the temple that was owned by high caste brahmin priests. That blew up as a political issue. A high caste educated member of parliament by the name of Sundaralingam supported the priest. The Communist party supported the Low cate people. Violence was instigated by the high caste crowd. The government agent of Jaffna at the time was a civil servant a Burger by the name of Vernon. He was an impartial efficient administrator. He directed the police superintendent by the name Sundararajan to give protection to the low caste people who wanted to enter the temple and pray. They argued that Murugan the god of Veddah is the god for all castes. Vernon commented sarcastically the crisis at Mavittapuram is a battle between two Suns referring to the MP and the Police superintendent. Moreover, Murugan married Valli a Veddah girl Later the issue was resolved by the verdict by the judiciary.

They are a popular tea stall by the name Aiyppan Tea corner. They served different varieties of tea with goat milk. Jeevan remembered people seated on a bench opposite that tea stall gossiping. Different varieties of bananas were sold in that shop.

When Jeevan went to the town that tea stall was not there. In that location, there was a saree shop. Jeeva was surprised to see a shop for computer games. That shop was well sponsored by the younger generation.

A jewelry shop by the name of Ambika Jewelers was an addition to the shops. The Jewelers also function as pawn brokers. Framers can obtain short terms cash loans by pawning your jewelry or gold. The Pawnbroker lends cash based on the value of your security deposit and charges interest daily.

After the independence, Jeevan remembered there was only the Bank of Ceylon with three staff who worked there. At that time Jeevan left the island People's Bank too and opened a Branch in Chunnkam. Now after forty years three more banks have appeared in Chunnkam. It may be due to factories and hotels appearing in Valigamam. Moreover, expatriate Tamils send money to their families through the Banks.

*****

CHAPTER SIXTEEN

VISALAATCHI

On the Manipay road from Uduvil, within a quarter of an acre, the small stone house of Visalaatchi is located.

Before Jeevan left for Canada, Visalaatchi had a Dosai take-out shop inside the Chunnkam market and was married to Victor. Her food shop was well catered by the shop owners inside the market and their customers. Victor was a driver at Uduvil Girl's college. This college is one of the oldest colleges built during Dutch rule. Jeevan met Victor only twice at the market at Visalaatchi's take-out shop. Victor could speak English.

****

Jeevan knocked at Visalaatchi's house door. A woman in her late twenties opened the door. She was slim, tall, and looked like Victor in appearance.

"Who are you, Aiyah? Whom do you want to see? " the woman asked.

" Is this Visalaatchi's house?"

"Yes. This is her house. Who are you"?

"I am Doctor Jeevan, the son of Mudaliyar Murugesu. Please tell your mother that I have come to meet her. "

When Visalaatchi heard Jeevan's voice and Mudaliyar Murugesu's name, Visalaatchi said to her daughter " Melani tell Thamby Jeevan to come in and sit down. I will be there in a few minutes."

" Please come in and sit Aiyah. My mother is busy, she will be here soon, "said Melani, Visalaatchi's daughter.

Jeevan went and sat on the chair. There was a dining table and a few chairs.

Victor's photo was hanging on the wall next to the Jesus Christ photo.

In a few minutes, Visalatchi came from the kitchen to the hall.

" I am sorry Thambi. I was busy cooking. I am very much delighted to see you after many years. Your appearance has changed. When did you come from Canada? Did your family come with you?"

Jeevan noted that there was not much change in Visalatchi's appearance. She had the same smile as before. Jeevan saw her after forty years.

" No Aachi, my family did not come with me. I came to sort out my land matters."

" Why did you not come to do the rites for your parent's funeral? You are their only son."

Jeevan gave the same explanation he gave to the cemetery keeper to Visalatchi.

"Why is it that your family did not come with you?"

"Aachi it is a quick trip for me to sort out the will. My wife and both children are working, and as such, they could not get leave. Is the lady who opened the door your daughter?".

" Yes, she is my only daughter. Her name is Melanie Nesamani. She was born many years after I got married. She is a music teacher in Uduvil Girls College ", Visalatchi replied.

" Aachi, is your husband Victor not living now?" I only met him twice in the market. Your daughter is tall as him ."

"My husband Victor worked for a few years as a driver at the Uduvil girl's College and then went to Dubai as a driver for an American company. One day while driving on his company business, he met with an accident and died. Since it was not his fault, I received some insurance money. With that money, I was able to educate my daughter and renovate my house and paid all my debts. He never smoked and drank liqueur All he wanted was delicious food. "

"Visalatchi, are you still selling Dosa, idly .appam"?

" After the army attacked the market, I did not want to have a shop in the market. I prepare food from home and give it to customers who order. They come and collect the food."

"Now I understand why you're doing business from home. Aachi the dosa hoppers and the food you prepare taste good. I missed your meal for the last forty years."

" Jeevan, I understand you. There is a significant difference between the food you eat in Canada and here. I doubt you get a variety of traditional delicious Jaffna food in Canada."

"That's true Aachi It is a mechanical life in Canada. Unlike in the villages here, there, the people do not help each other. There are Sri Lankan take-out shops, but the quality of food is not good. They keep the food in the fridge and warm and sell it. There is no room for progress for educated Tamils in this country. That is why I migrated to Canada after the riots in this country. Like me, many professionals migrated after the war. Now the economy is deteriorating in this country. Educated people want to get out of this country."

" True Thambi. The prices of all food items have gone up. I cook the food using firewood and in clay pots. I know that like you .many educated Tamils migrated to different countries. I must make a living and work hard at this age. Now that you have come to my house, I will prepare Jaffna's favorite dishes for you."

"Aachi, I notice that you follow the traditional cooking using firewood and utensils such as Ural, Ulakai, Ammi, kulavi, Sullagu, etc. . They are the traditional utensils used for cooking in villages here. We had in our house those Jaffna traditional utensils used for cooking.

My mother used clay pots and firewood for cooking. We do not find them in Canada. Curry levees spices are expensive. We use s aluminum vessels, Mixer, Gas cooker, and Refrigerator. We cook and keep them for days in the refrigerator. We take them, out and warm them in the microwave oven and eat. "

" Jeevan that is not good for health. At times you may get food poisoning. The foreign tourists who come to this village love to eat Jaffna traditional food.

They love Jaffna mangoes, bananas, and jack fruit. Two tourist guides are known to me, and they bring the tourists here to enjoy the food prepared by me. I also serve them palmyra toddy. They sit on a mat and enjoy eating on a banana leaf. They love to eat with their hands. They wash their hands and legs before eating. They say it is very tasty to eat on a banana leaf."

"Aachi, you cannot converse in English. How do you communicate with foreign tourists?

" Melani can speak English. So, she is my interpreter."

Jeevan looked at Melani and asked her what grade she got for her ordinary level exam

" Aiyah, I got distinctions in English, Math, Music, and Tamil. I am, a trained Music teacher. I play the violin."

" I am glad to hear that, Melani. So, you are helping your mother to earn dollars."

" At times, the tourist give gifts. They gave me a small camera"

" I am glad to hear that. Can you sing a song for me?"

Melani went to the bedroom, brought her violin, and sang the Uduvil girl's college anthem. At Jeevan's request, she sang M S Subbalakshmi's song "The song that comes on the wind."

from the old film Meera

"That was my mother's favorite song. Aachi, you have a talented daughter. You should find a matching partner for her."

" Thamby Jeevan, she wants to marry her boyfriend, Ramanan. He is a flute player? He is a Hindu. We are Chrisman's. That is why I am hesitating to agree to her marrying Ramanan. Ramanan is a teacher at Jaffna college at Vaddukootai."

" Aachi these days region and caste and ethnicity are no barriers. I know many Tamils have married Sinhalese. Better you agree to her choice. You love to see a grandchild soon. I will give you some cash to meet her marriage expenses." Jeevan gave Thirty thousand rupees to Visalaatchi for her daughter's marriage."

"Thambi Jeevan you are so generous like your father. He once helped me in my marriage to Victor."

"I love to help people whom I love. I will go for a walk in the paddy fields in the village and come back in two hours for dinner."

" That time is more than enough to get ready with the food you like. After visiting me where are you planning to go?"

"I want to visit Temple dancer Chinthamani. I liked her dancing. Unfortunately, she had an affair with the Changanai village rowdy Maniam.

"One time she was a slim lady. Many rich village people wanted to marry her. But Maniam was an obstacle to her marriage, she conceived through Maniam a married man. Now she has a beautiful daughter, I do not like Chinthamani."

"Aachi I will go out and come back in two hours to enjoy your Dosai, and hoppers with sambol, and fish curry."

Jeevan left Visalatchi's and visited the

Maruthady Pillayar temple. And Greens hospital

The Green Memorial Hospital is a non-profit hospital in Manipay, Sri Lanka. It was founded by Dr. Samuel Fisk Green in 1848. It is a charitable hospital run by the Jaffna Diocese of the Church of South India This hospital was the first medical school in Ceylon (now Sri Lanka) and was used by Dr. Green to train more than sixty locals as doctors during his 30-year tenure in Ceylon as part of the American Ceylon Mission. Green Memorial Hospital is the second oldest teaching hospital in South Asia.

Jeevan returned after two hours.

****

After enjoying a delicious dinner Jeevan left in a three-wheeler to Margosa lodge. It was almost eight pm. He had a shower and went to bed, The next day after breakfast he will be visiting Chinthamani and his former Maths teacher Ganapathy with Rajan's uncle in his car to the Alavetty village.

He also wanted to see the Valukai river that flows through Alavetty, a fertile village. Rajan knew that there was a poet by the name of Rudramoorthy from that village.

After visiting his math teacher, his next visit will be to the house of the drama teacher Chornalingam and the Zoology teacher. The day after these visits Jeevan planned to spend the full day with Rathydevi.

*****

CHAPTER SEVENTEEN

THE DANCER CHINTHAMANI

After a good night's sleep, at six am Jeevan was put by the hotel boy. He had a quick shower, dressed up, and had breakfast. He ate string hoppers with gravy and Maldive fish sambol along with coffee. There were sliced mangoes for dessert. Jeevan was ready at nine am waiting for Rajan's uncle's arrival.

Rajan was there at the appointed time. Both left for Chankanai to visit Chinthamani. Rajan did not like that trip. He never liked Chintamani as she had an illegal love affair with a married man. Maniam from Changanai village.

Maniam was a rowdy from Chankanai. Rajan appeared in three cases of extortion of money by Maniam. In two cases he was fined heavily by the Judge in the third case he was sentenced to six months in jail. Rajan was aware of the illegal relationship between the temple dancer Chinthamani and Maniam.

Maniam was married to Kavitha the sister of his maternal uncle. Kavitha complained to Rajan about her husband Maniyam's love affair with Chintamani. Kavitha also complained that the jewelry given as dowry to her by her parents was forcibly taken by her husband to be given to his lover. When Rajan received the complaint from Kavitha, he called Maniam to his office and advised him to give up his relationship with Chinthamani and return the jewelers to his wife. Maniam did not like his advice. He warned Rajan not to interfere in his matter.

Rajan later spoke to Chintamani and requested her not to have a relationship with Maniam.

Chinthamani told him that she was intimidated by Maniam to have sex with him and to love him only. Through fear, she had an affair with Maniam.

While driving the car to Chankanai village where Chintamani's house is in a lane near the Changanai market, Rajan narrated the affair between Chintamani a Maniam to Jeevan

After listening to Rajan. Jeevan said "Uncle Rajan when I was a student I liked dancing, music, and drama. I was participating in two dramas staged by the Chornlaingam master's drama group. Chornlaingam's master spoke high of Chintamani's dancing capability. Hence, I decided to go to a temple festival and see her dancing. I went to see the dance without the permission of my father."

"Did you enjoy her dance at the temple festival?"

" Yes, I was impressed by her movements and song. She had talent. Unfortunately, I was forced by Maniam to sit by his side and watch the dance. He told me whatever dance I want to watch he can order Chintamani to dance. As she was her lover, she will conduct his orders.

I did not like what he said. There was arrogance in the way he spoke. I wanted to leave the place immediately. He made me sit and watch all her dances.

After the dance was over, he told me he will be giving a lift to Chinthamani, and I too can join him in his car. I said that I have come on my bicycle with a friend of mine, as such I must go home with my friend.

Now that you told me that Maniam intimidated Chintamani to love him, I feel that we cannot blame her to be Maniyam's lover/

Mariam got the punishment for the bad Karma he accumulated and was killed by a student."

"It is true, I appeared as the student in the Maniyam's murder case. I argued that Maniam provoked the student as a result he threw a stone at him. The stone hit the temple which is located on the side of the head behind the eye between the forehead and the ear. By the impact of the stone Maniam fainted and died.

Moreover, I argued that he was a heart patent, and the death was due to a heart attack."

"Uncle let us not talk all these with Chinthamani when getting there If you like better you can stay in the car. I will see her and come back in an hour/"

" That is a good suggestion Jeevan," replied Rajan.

When they reached Chintamani's house. Rajan parked the car away from Chintamani's house. , Jeevan got down and went to meet Chinthamani.

****

At Chintamani's house, her daughter received Jeevan. She also looked pretty like her mother.

"Aiyah, may I know who you are "? She asked Jeevan.

"I am the son of Mudaliyar Murugesu. I have come to meet dancer Chintamani ".

Immediately she called her mother and spoke.

"A person by the name of Jeevan, the son of Mudaliyar Murugesu, has come to meet you Ammah."

An old woman's voice from a room said immediately

"I know him. Bring him immediately."

Jeevan went to the room where Chintamani was lying on a bed.

She was lying paralyzed. Her beauty had disappeared. Wrinkles on her face and lost partly her eyesight.

"Sit in that chair, Jeevan. See my condition I am paying for my karma " she said with tears in her eyes.

" What happened to you Chinthamani. I heard your lover was killed by a student because Maniam bullied him."

" He was killed at a time when you were not in Chunnkam.

I am of the view that t god punished him for what he did for me and many villagers. Your father advised him to change his habits. He never listened to him. Your father knew that I did not love him. One day I confessed to your father about my lover Manoharan. Manoharan was a Nadaswaram player from Alavetty. Maniam came to know about my lover. He threatened him that he will kill him. To save his life Manoharan left for south India.

To be true I did not love Maniam. He behaved like a thug. He threatened and had sex with me. He gave me this child who is standing near you."

Jeevan was shocked to hear her pathetic story He turned towards the girl and asked Chintamani's daughter" What is your name?"

"She is Radha. She has not seen her father's face. He was killed when this girl was in my womb. It is good that she did not see the face of the man who raped and ruined the Jeevan of her mother," Chintamani replied to Jeevan his question.

Radha did not say a word. she was looking at the ground

"What are you doing now Radha?" Jeevan asked her,

" Studying nursing," she replied in a soft voice

" Who is financing your studies"?

" Maniyam's legal wife's son Kannan is financing her studies. He has no sisters. He and her mother Kavitha loves this girl. They both regret the sins caused by Maniam. Kannan is living in Germany He sends money for his mother and my daughter and me. He is just the opposite of his father in character, Even Kavitha is a good-hearted lady. I told her my whole story. She said to me that it was not my mistake. She blamed her husband," replied Chinthamani.

" What happened to his properties? Did you get any share after his death?"

"The house and half an acre of land he had gone to his wife Kavitha. I have no right to claim it as I did not marry him."

"I Understand your situation now. Keep this cash for the education of your daughter, She and Kannan will look after you " Jeevan gave her twenty-five thousand rupees.

Thank you, Jeevan, for the kind donation. Would you like to have tea? I will ask Radha to prepare it for you."

" Don't worry Chintamani It is time for me to go as I have two more places to visit."

" Ok, Jeevan please our best wishes to your family," Chintamani said.

Jeevan came out of the house and walked toward the car.

"Jeevan how was your meeting with Chinthamani.? Rajan asked him.

Her condition I pathetic. She lost her beauty. She told me her full story I pity her. She never loved Maniam. He forced her to have affair with him. Chintamani has a pretty daughter."

" She must pay for Karma. Let us go to Alavetty to meet your math master," said Rajan.

****

CHAPTER EIGHTEEN

MATH'S TEACHER GANAPATHY

Rajan drove to Alavetty to meet Ganapathi, the math's master Ganapathy who taught Jeevan. While traveling in the car Jeevan said,

" Uncle Rajan Ganapati Master was a famous Math's at that time I was studying at Skandvordaya college.

He was a good Physics teacher too. He graduated from Tiruchirappalli Saint Joseph College in Tamil Nadu. He had an excellent memory. He taught Chess to many students. The math problems he gave were a challenge to us the students. I scored the highest marks in Maths in his class. I solved difficult geometry problems. He once told me " Jeevan you are very good at Math, you should do Engineering."

I replied to him "Master, my parents wanted me to be a doctor."

He asked me the reason

I told him that it was because my dad's uncle's son was a doctor who, studied in Sri Lanka and moved to London after working for a few years."

Ganapathy's master never punished students but gave them more homework. He did not have a punished student like the other teachers

He had a passion for mathematics as well as Tamil.

" He narrated a few parodies in his class which I still remember in my mind"

"What is the parody, Jeevan?"

" Add revenue, subtract expenses.

Never think that zero has no value. It has more value than negative

numbers. The railway line is an example of a Parallel line.

Universe has Infinity space."

" Very interesting quotes."

Ganapathy Master comes to Skandvordaya College from Alavetty in an old bicycle. He brings his lunch as well. He would arrive half an hour

early to college, spends his time correcting the files of the students who had done their homework, and then returns to class on time.

He always had a pen in the pocket of his short-sleeve shirt. He had holy ash on his forehead. He had a habit of using tobacco snuff.

I had been to his house twice. It was an old house. There was a mango tree near the gate." Jeevan narrated to Rajan his experience with his math teacher.

****

As Jeevan entered the Maths teacher's house, he remembered the room in the front verandah where he gave tuitions.

The blackboard and the few chairs and tables were still there.

Rajan said " It is OK Jeevan take your time. I like to see the Valukai river which flows half a kilo metro from here. It was a canal built from Taipei to Araly 16 miles long. It supplies water to paddy fields in Alavetty"

As Jeevan walked in the garden, he remembered the ferocious dog Veeran Ganapathy had. Thank God there is no dog now. The mango tree is not to be seen. As he stepped onto the verandah, he saw the room with a black brad where Ganapathy's grave tuitions. The Blackboard is still there, but the table and chairs were missing.

Jeevan knocked at the door. Gammopathy teacher's wife opened the door

Jeevan recognized her.

" Can you recognize me Sundari aunty?"

Sundari took a few seconds to recognize Jeevan

and said "Yes, I remember you. You are my husband's favorite student Jeevan, He wanted you to become an engineer, but you became a doctor.

Your father Mudaliyar Murugesu is my husband's good friend. Your father helped my husband to get my son's birth certificate. Please come in and be seated. What do you like to drink, Buttermilk, Tea, or Coffee?"

" Don't worry about the drink aunty. I came to see Ganapathy's teacher and you. Now I am working in Canada as a doctor., I have come after many years to Chunnkam to settle my will matters."

Jeevan saw Ganapathy's teacher in an easy chair, busy writing in an exercise book. there were papers all around the easy chair. Ganapathy lifted his head and looked at Jeevan but did not welcome him or identify him. He then continued writing in the notebook. Jeevan was surprised by his behavior.

' Look Jeevan did you see the situation of my husband. His memories have vanished. He is suffering from Alzheimer's. He cannot identify anyone. He behaves like a child. That is why he did not welcome you."

" I understand aunty. Many people get this disease at old age. Aunty when did this start?"

" He started losing his memory a few years back. One day he went to the Temple and did not return Luckily a person known to our family brought him home and said that my husband lost his way. That was the starting point.

Another day he went to buy some groceries. When he returned, he came without the items he bought? Another day he was about to leave the house with only one slipper.

"Where are your son Murali and daughter Devaki?"

"Murali passed out as an Engineer and migrated to London Daughter got married to my brother's son and migrated to Australia.' We both could not migrate to those countries because of Ganapathy's master's health condition. They send money for our existence and

doctors' expenses. He gets his pension.

"Sundari aunty, can I see what he is writing?"

"Why not? but do not ask him any questions. He will not reply to your questions. He will only stare at you."

Jeevan went and took the papers on the ground and looked at them There were geometric shapes and figures.

Jeevan stood close to him and said "Ganapathy master I am Jeevan your favorite student I have come to see you. Ganapathy did not lift his head and reply to Jeevan. Jeevan knew that Ganapathy's master is in an advanced stage of Alzheimer's.

"Sundari Aunty who feeds him and takes him to the toilet and baths him?"

" We pay a nurse to come home and nurse him. I am too old to take care of him. I get money from Devaki in Australia and Som Murali from London to pay for the nurse. My son and daughter did not want their father to be admitted to a senior's home. Both come once a year with their family to see him. I am happy that I have two good children,"

"That is a good decision by your children aunty. But please do not stress out and fall sick. Do you cook at this old age?"

"Oh no. A servant woman cones daily and does cooking, I pay her."

Jeevan saw the books used by his teacher in an almirah.

"Can I have a look at those books' aunty?"

"Why not, here is the key. I never opened the almirah, there may be ` dust."

Jeevan opened the almirah and many Maths Physics books. He also saw Tamil historical novels written by his favorite writer Kalki Krishnamoorthy. He cleaned the dust that was collected on the books. The Physics book Parker and Nelson was there He also noticed basic Arithmetic, Calculus, Trigonometry, Geometry, Algebra, and Applied mathematics by Loney. In every book, his teacher had signed and dated. Some books go back to the fifties. After dusting, Jeevan arranged the books.

He gave the key back to Sundari.

" Aunty, it is pleasure to see his signature in each of those books. Some books take my memory back to about fifty years. It is a pity that the Ganapathi master is not able to recognize me. Please keep these fifty thousand rupees as my contribution to buy medicines and healthy food for both of you

"Jeevan. I receive from my children money. Thank God I have no shortage of money to look after my husband."

"It is OK aunty Keep this money as my contribution to the education he gave me."

Sundari could not refuse the money Jeevan gave. She thanked him.

"Ok, Aunty it is time for me to go I came in Rajan's uncle's car he will be waiting for me."

Before leaving Jeevan went to the easy chair where Ganapathy was seated and busy writing. Jeevan took Ganapathy's right hand and kissed it. Teras dropped from Jeevan's eyes as he could not control

his emotions.

Sundari, wife of Ganapathy stood shocked when she noted the way Jeevan bid goodbye to his Math teacher Ganapathy.

*****

CHAPTER NINETEEN

THE DRAMA TEACHER CHORNALINGAM

From Alavetty Rajan drove his car to Anaikottai where Chornalingam's master's house is located.

On the route to Anaikottai Rajan who was

interested in Archaeology said "Jeevan we are going to a village of archeological heritage"

" Uncle please explain it to me."

"Anaikottai is a town located in Valikamam, Southwest. Cultural remains were found during excavations in this village. During excavations in Anaikottai emblems of Paleolithic people were found in two places. Two Urn centers were found on a mound ten feet apart and four feet high at set intervals as well. The Brahmi-engraved pottery found at Anaikottai is based on Lakshmi coins and Roman pottery, which confirms that two urns with emblems belonged to these Paleolithic people dating back to 2,300 years ago. The bronze seal found near the head of the skeleton is of great historical significance. It dates to the third century BC. Elephants were once kept in nests there during the reign of the king. Hence the name Anaikottai.

So, in the past it was an important business area, now this village is popular for sesame oil." said Rajan. The village is located a few Km along the Jaffna – Manipay road.

" Uncle you are interested in archelogy, but I am interested in drama, music, and dance My school teacher Chornalingam is an expert in rural arts. He is also famous for performing folk songs. He is living

in this village. Like Alavetty village this village also produced poets, and artistic professionals specializing in folk drama and music."

****

Rajan stopped his car at a shop to inquire about the location of the Chornalingam master's house. The shopkeepers said that it is a tiled house

with a green color gate located about a quarter km down the lane next to the shop. The lane was broad enough for a car to travel.

When they both reached the house of Chornalingam Master, a dog barked. Immediately someone from the house shouted,

"Jimmy, be quiet,"

The dog stopped barking and ran into the house.

Jeevan went and knocked on the door of the house. A 16-year-old boy came and opened the door and asked, "Whom do you want to see Aiyah?"

Jeevan replied, "Is this Chornalingam master's house?"

"Yes, Aiyah" the boy replied.

"We have come to see him. Please go and inform him that Mudaliyar Murugesu's son Jeevan has come with lawyer Rajan to see him."

"Master is busy repairing the drum that is used in dramas. I will inform him

that you both have come to see him."

The boy went into the house after requesting them both to sit on the chairs on the verandah.

From the room, they heard the noise of the drum being repaired. In a few minutes, Chornlaingam's master came out to the verandah. He immediately recognized Jeevan.

"Aren't you Mudaliyar Murugesu's son Jeevan, who acted in two dramas staged by my group when you were a student at Skanda?"

" I am. He is my uncle's lawyer Rajan. How are you keeping master? It looks like you are still active in staging dramas ."

" I am incredibly happy to see you Jeevan after many years I attended your parent's funeral. I heard from some teachers that after qualifying as a doctor you worked in some hospitals in the south and you were affected by ethnic riot and migrated to Canada."

" That is a true master. I could not come to my parent's funeral because there was an Eelam war for thirty years."

" I can understand your reason. It was a good decision for you. Are you working as a doctor In Canada?"

" Yes, master. It was a requirement to pass a certain mediçal exam to be accepted as a doctor to work in that country. I passed within two years after going to Canada and started working. I am married to a Tamil from Malaysia and have a son and a daughter. I came alone to sort out legal issues associated with the will written by my parents," Jeevan replied.

" I remember you in two dramas staged by me when you were a student. Since you did not get permission from your father to act, I spoke to him and got the permission. He was a good man. He never liked drama."

"Master, are you still writing verses for village dramas and playing the harmonium."

" I am now 82 years old. I will be living for a few more years. Until I die, I will never forget drama and music."

Jeevan enjoyed talking to him about archery puppetry and false horse caricature.

"Thambi Jeevan these folk are still there in Tamil Nadu because of the cinema. You would have seen the movie Karakattakkaran and Sangamam, from those two films you can understand how much support is there for

folk art in that country. Unfortunately, there is not much support for folk music and art in our towns now. There is still support for it in Eastern Sri Lanka ."

"What you are saying is a true master. The present young community in Jaffna loves western music and dance because of the culture and changes in traditions time. With digital technology coming in, there is a change in acting music and drama."

"Even the sesame oil shop at the top of the lane was a small many years ago. After the owner's son migrated to France, he sent

money to expand the shop to sell other types of oils and grocery

items. "

" Master, I remember you teaching me how to act in a folk drama. In the first drama acted, I had a stage fear, but with your guidance, I did well."

" Jeevan, I have in my album the photos of the two dramas you acted."

Jeevan was surprised to hear what the Chornalingam master said.

" Master I'm eager to see those pictures and I'll take a few of them with me if you don't mind."

" Why not Jeevan. You may like to show the photos to your family ."

.He immediately got up and went to his room and brought

the album that contained two pictures in which Jeevan acted. Chornlaingam gave those photos to Jeevan, and Jeevan thanked him for the photos.

Jeevan saw a broken harmonium in the corner of the room

Jeevan asked him "What master have you broken your harmonium you were using "?

He said, " That was broken for almost six months. I have no money to fix it."

Jeevan immediately said, "Master, you do not have to worry about anything. Keep this money as my gift for your artistic passion. Buy a new harmonium with this money."

" My dear Jeevan, you have given me a large amount of money. I know you can afford it as you are a Doctor in Canada. Your love for drama and music is still there in you I am happy to accept your donation ."

Chornlaingam's master then persuaded Jeevan and Rajan to

have lunch with him. Jeevan knows that he does not eat meat. But he often drank some local liquor.

When having lunch Jeevan asked, " Master who is this boy "?

Chornlaingam replied to Jeevan with a smile

"Jeevan, this boy's parents died during the Eelam war. He became an orphan; I saw him singing in a drama. I liked him so I adopted him as my grandson ."

"What's his name, master?" Jeevan asked

"His parents gave him the name was Maheswaran, but I changed the name to Balan".

" Short name. Easy to remember".

"Jeevan, the art and culture of a country is the best tool to discipline the community. Art is not only a means of entertainment but also a means of communication and a cultural tool. Art is an expression of mental feelings. Especially the theatrical arts are related to our soil and us. Reflecting our heritage and deep roots. Art is an excellent tool for social development and motivation.

The beliefs, thoughts, ideas, and customs of our ancestors can be discerned through folk art. These arts are the document of society. It is these rural arts that have become the medium of communication and the repository of customary culture. " Chornalingam said

Rajan and Jeevan spoke to the master's wife thanking her for the food prepared by her. Both left for Chunnkam in the evening.

*** **

CHAPTER TWENTY

THE ZOOLOGY TEACHER

Jeevan was keen on meeting his Zoology teacher, Short Sundaralingam. He was called Short Sundar as there was a history teacher by the same name Tall Sundar. who was a six-footer, During Jeevan's school days each schoolteacher is given a nickname based on appearance and their behavior in the class?

Short Sundar taught Jeevan zoology and Botany in Advanced Level class. He was an excellent teacher. His hometown was Kondavil, a village south of Chunnakam. Short Sundar studied at St Joseph's college Tiruchirappalli and got a first-class degree in biological science. He traveled daily to school by bicycle from Kondavil. Jeevan's father helped the Short Sundar teacher to get his daughter Mangai's birth certificate from the Jaffna kachcheri. Jeevan was Short Sundar's favorite student.

Sundaralingam master was an expert in narrating interesting jokes and Jataka stories about animals. Jeevan hated cockroaches and frogs but was interested in learning about flowers and plants. One day Jeevan asked the teacher the question " master why do flowers have assorted colors"?

"Good question Jeevan. The most common pigments in flowers come in the form of anthocyanins. These pigments range in color from white to red to blue to yellow to purple and even black and brown. A different kind of pigment class is made up of carotenoids. Carotenoids are responsible for some yellows, orange, and red colour flowers. The number of light flowers receives while they grow, the temperature of the environment around them, and even the pH level of the soil in which they grow can affect their coloration. Another factor is stress from the environment. This stress can include drought or a flood or even a lack of nutrition in the soil, all of which can dampen the coloration of flowers. And then, of course, there is the visual that the eye and brain form together: humans can view all colors in the visible spectrum. Every human perceives color differently, so a red rose may appear more vibrant to one person while it appears more muted to another. Beauty and color are in the eye of the beholder."

There was a Zoology practical class. Sundar's teacher explained to them how to dissect frogs and cockroaches. These two are hated by Jeevan.

The students were asked by the teacher to bring a frog for dissection. Jeevan was scared to catch a frog. He asked his servant to catch a frog from a pond and bottle it and give it to him to be taken to practical class. He remembered that experience even today.

Even to enter medical college there was a test on dissection. The practical test at the university was stopped because there were no good labs in village schools.

Sundaralingam Master once told Jeevan, " Jeevan, if you want to be a doctor, at medical college, you must know about the several parts of the human body. At the exam, you may have to dissect dead bodies ."

Jeevan recalled what the Zoology teacher said while studying at the Colombo Medical College

Sundaralingam master's bicycle often gave problems. Jeevan took it to the repair shop for repair and returns it to him.

Master had a son and a daughter. Uncle Rajan told Jeevan that when a Zoology teacher's son was studying at the University of Peradeniya, he fell in love with a Singhalese girl who studied with him, He married her. Sundar's master did not like his son Ranjan marrying a Singhalese as such Ranjan's family did not have any contact with Sundaralingam's family. Ranjan family lived in Kandy.

Sundar teacher's wife Mangai was a good singer. She sang movie songs. She sang songs from the Tamil film Meera. Sundar was the one who fell in love with her when he gave the tuition to her. Mamgai's parents initially objected to the love affair. Jeevan's father mediated and arranged the marriage between Sundar and Mangai then. Jeevan's father Mudaliyar Murugesu was the witness to their marriage.

*****

When Jeevan returned to the village, he could not meet the Sundaralingam teacher, as he died a few years ago. When Jeevan inquired about him, Rajan Uncle said that after the death of his teacher, his wife Mangai emigrated with her daughter Sumathy to Australia.

At the Saraswathi Bookstore in Chunnakam market, Jeevan asked the Book shop owner if there is a zoology book written by the Sundaralingam Master for the A/L.

"Are you new to this town?" the book shop owner asked Jeevan.

Jeevan smiled and asked, "I have studied under Sundaralingam teacher. I used the master Sundaralingam Zoology book. I am Dr. Jeevan, the son of Mudaliyar Murugesu. I have returned to Chunnkam from Canada after many years. That is why you do not know me."

"Doctor forgive me. I bought this shop from the previous owner only a few years back. I have the sixth edition of the Zoology book written by late Sundaralingam."

"Please give me three copies of the book."

"Why Doctor, you require three copies"?

"I want to show my kids the book I used at the college. I want to give other two copies to his students who are now in Canada. They will love to have the book."

The book contained a picture of Sunder Master taken when he was a young handsome man. Jeevan understood why his wife Mangai fell in love with him.

*****

CHAPTER TWENTY-ONE

RATHYDEVI

Rathydevi

Rathydevi, the sister of Jeevan's friend Ravi, was known by many students as a village beauty during her school days. Born in a rich family, she studied at the Uduvil girl's College. She traveled to the college from Chunnakam in a bow cart. She grew up in parental control. Overseer Nadarajah is a family friend of Mudaliyar Murugesu. Murugesu helped Nadarajah to get the contracts to repair roads in many villages in Valigamam. Nadarajah's wife Rajamma had a good friendship with Jeevan's mother Nallanachiyar. Jeevan visited Nadarajah's house several times with his mother.

"Naachiyar, when your son becomes a doctor, I wish that you have no objection to my daughter Rathy marrying your son" Rajamma once said.

" I and my husband like your pretty. intelligent, pious daughter Rathy. She is an ideal match for my son. But only time and God will decide their marriage Rajamma ." replied Jeevan's mother.

Jeevan's mother was always careful in promising anything to her friend. Jeevan developed a liking for Rathy when he heard what his mother said. He knew that Rathy too likes him. Jeevan would talk to her about her studies. Jeevan excelled in three subjects: Zoology, Botany, and Chemistry. Rathy cleared her doubts on those subjects through Jeevan.

Jeevan gives a lift in his bicycle to Ravi after school and drops his friend Ravi at his home. He makes use of that opportunity to meet Rathy and spends time talking to her. Her parents never objected to it. A love affair bloomed between them. After Jeevan entered medical college in Colombo his chances to meet Rathy were reduced. Only when he goes to Chunnkam during the holidays does he visits Rathy's house with his mother Nallanachiyar.

Jeevan's parents and Rathy's parents agreed to arrange the marriage between Jeevan and Rathy. The riots and the Eelam war toppled their decision. as Jeevan migrated to Canada. He could not return to his village. In Canada, circumstances forced him to marry Malini the Malaysian Tamil nurse. Rathy decided not to marry anyone other than Jeevan. Incidents such as the death of her brother Ravi and her parents isolated her. She lost contact with Jeevan. She knew that Jeevan is married and had two children.

****

Jeevan asked, "Uncle Rajan, where is Rathy now?

"She retired as a Teacher at Uduvil girl's college and now manages a Senior's home in Uduvil. Do you want to go and meet her?"

Jeevan said, "Yes Uncle. I want to meet her and apologize for disappointing her . Fate has cheated both of us. and I will ask her whether she can take charge of the senior home which I am planning to start,".

" Your idea is good. I wish that she will agree to it. I will take you to meet her. It is Hendy's senior's home in Uduvil, and she manages it. But I do not know if she will leave that home and come to manage your senior's home. Talk to her and convince her. Good luck."

Jeevan asked, "Uncle is she not married"?

"Why are you asking that question Jeevan? When you were in Canada my cousin's son who works as an Engineer in London, wanted to marry her. She refused to marry him. I do not know what was in her mind and why she refused to marry."

Jeevan felt sorry about her living unmarried.

Rajan took Jeevan in his car to the Senior's home in Uduvil for which Rathy is the Administratrix,

As he was driving, Rajan asked, "Do you know how Jeevan Uduvil got its name?"

"I don't know Uncle"

A long time back the name Uduvil came from the presence of thorny trees called Udu around a tank in the town. Vil in Tamil means tank. The Sinhalese say that Mahayana Buddhist monks from Tamil Nadu lived in this town during the time of Manimekalai. "

Before meeting Rathy, Jeevan bought a red rose to be given to Rathy, He knew that Rathy loves roses.

At the security point of the Handy Senior's home, Rajan told the security guard that they both have come to meet Rathy the lady in charge of the Senior's home.

The security guard took them to the office. They both saw at a distance Rathy talking to a lady. Jeevan could not believe that even though she was told she looked beautiful, slim in look. Her beautiful eyes added to her beauty. When she saw Jeevan, she was in shock. , It took a minute for her to say " Hello Jeevan is it you?

"Yes, Rathy I am Dr. Jeevan yours and your brother Ravi's friend. Mudaliyar Murugesu's son. The friend from whom you got help in Chemistry. "

She got up from her seat and walked toward Jeevan to receive him.

"Jeevan, when did you come from Canada to Chunnakam?"

"It has been a few days since I arrived, Rathy."

Jeevan gave the red rose to Rathy and said " Rathy I bought this rose for you. I know that you like roses"

"Thank you for the red rose. I am happy to know that you still remember that I like a red rose."

"Yes, Rathy, I remember you had a red rose plant in your house."

"Let us not talk about that house. It was destroyed during the war."

" I am sorry to hear that." Jeevan apologized.

" I never expected that you will come back to Chunnakam. Did you come with your family"?

"No, Rathy. I came to sort out the will that was written in my name by my parents. Uncle Rajan told me about your parents and your brother Ravi. My heartfelt condolences to you. Like Ravi, I heard that many students joined the Tamil Tiger movement because they could not enter the University I will be returning to Canada in a week" Jeevan said holding her hands.

She liked the touch of Jeevan after many years. Her eyes fluttered. She stood in silence.

" Dear Jeevan, why did you leave us all without telling us and go to Canada? "

"What can I do Rathy? I emigrated due to ethnic riots in Sri Lanka. I could not continue to work in Sri Lanka. I worked at the Panadura Hospital when the mobs attacked my house. I am lucky to have escaped death. I expected Ravi to enter the University, but his failure made him join the Tamil liberation movement."

She went silent. Jeevan also did not want to talk further about Ravi. He knew that Rathy is missing her loving brother.

"Jeevan, my parents did not like my brother joining the Tamil Tiger movement. Ravi died in the battle of Poonakari as a Captain. I still remember you going to college on your Raleigh bicycle with my brother Ravi. Both of you went to the Wellington Theater at Jaffna to watch Tamil movies. You and he played cricket together. After school, you dropped Ravi at our house and talked to me. Those are the happy old days. After you left us and went to Canada, I thought that you will return after a few years and marry me. I waited for many years. I could not raze you from my memory. Fate has created us."

" Rathy, during school days, I and Ravi engraved both our names and your name in the Neem tree in the cemetery. I went and checked to see whether the names are there."

" What did you see Jeevan?"

" The names are still there engraved with the date. I took a photograph of it to show it to my family."

" Ravi said to me that before you engraved my name. He told me that you got his permission to engrave it. Ravi was aware of our close relationship. He wanted you to become his brother-in-law, " Rathy said.

" Rathy why are you not married"?

She was silent for a few seconds and then said, " Jeevan you know the answer."

" Rathy at old age you should have a partner to care for you."

"In my heart, there is a place for one man and that is you only. I cannot allow anyone to occupy that place."

Jeevan was shocked to hear that reply from Rathy.

" After going to Canada, I was more concerned about qualifying as a doctor. It was a big mistake I made. I should have gotten married to you and taken you with me to Canada."?

" I heard that you got married to a Tamil girl;"

"Yes, Rathy. I fell in love with and married a Malaysian Tamil girl. Her name is Malini, a nurse in the hospital where I worked in Canada. Her `parents' ancestry is from Urumpirai not too far from Chunnakam. Her paternal grandfather worked as a Postmaster in Malaysia during the British period.

"How many children do you have now?"

"Two. Eldest son Romesh and a daughter Devi: "

" Why did you use part of my name for your daughter?"

" Whenever I call my daughter Devi, I could remember you?"

"It's your decision. What are they doing?"

"They both are working," Jeevan said

"I'm so happy to hear that, everything happens according to one's destiny," Rathy said.

Jeevan did not answer. Rathi looked at him and said: "It is better to talk about other things other than talking about this marriage and past Jeevan".

"Okay Rathy, I have a plan to start a Senior's home at our old house at Puthur road. I have to renovate the house ."

" Is that the reason why you came to Chunnakam?"

"Rathi, I came to Chunnakam to sort out the legal issues related to the will written in my name by my parents. They have written the house where we lived and the land and a paddy field in my name. There is my mother's Jewelry in the Bank safe. I am now a Canadian citizen as such I am not going to come back here and live with my family. My children will find it difficult to live in this society."

" So, what are you going to do with your assets? Are you going to sell them?" Rathy asked Jeevan.

" Oh no. It is my ancestry property. That is why I have planned to start a Senior home in the house I lived. You have been to my house several times with your parents and Ravi. It is a big house built in the Chettinad style. There are many bedrooms. We hardly used them."

" I know that that it is a big house. You may have to redesign it for a senior's home like this senior's home. In addition, you have a big garden in the front and back yard. There is a well with excellent quality water. It is an ideal place for a senior's home." Rathy said.

" I have a plan for this. With the help of Rajan and Chunnkam Alavetty Urelu village associations in Canada, we can have seniors such as Ganapathy Master. Chornlaingam Master Visalatchi and Chintamani in that Senior's home ."

" Are you the only one who is going to fund this?"

"Rather it is not me only. There are four Valigamam village associations in Canada. I have spoken to the Board of Directors of those associations. They have agreed to support this project."

"How many people will be there in that home"? Rathy asked.

"Initially twenty elderly people. After that, the number may be increased "

" What help you expect from me Jeevan?"

" I wish to know whether you can manage the Senior's home. As per the project plan, there will be an outhouse for the person who manages the home which is going to start. Uncle Rajan will assist you with any legal issues. You can select your staff. You have the experience of running a Senior home. I am going to finalize the building plans with a construction company. You too may join that meeting "

"Jeevan if I am going to look after the senior's home that you are going to start, I must find someone to look after this Senior's home. The seniors here love me. Managing two seniors' homes will be too much load for me. You know that I am not young as before."

"I will provide all financial help from Canada. You and Rajan's uncle can hire staff for the Senior home. "

After thinking for a while, she said, "Well, I cannot say a no to you provided Rajan should help me, "said Rathi.

Her response was very satisfying to Jeevan.

"Thanks, Rathy, for your agreement ."

" Don't mention, please. Jeevan, please bring your wife and two children one day to Chunnakam. I like to see them. "

"Rathi I will talk to them and try to send them to Chunnakam at least once. If possible, I will come with them. I will finish this initial work on this project and go back to Canada in a week. Rajan's uncle will deal with plan approval with the Chunnakam Town council. Do you need any help from me ?" Jeevan asked.

" You are a doctor in Canada it would be nice if you could do something to help this nursing home ".

"What help do you need?"

"If possible, help financially, to buy ten beds and build a bathroom," she said.

"Rathy, that is not a problem I will send you a check for one lakh of rupees immediately through Uncle Rajan. In whose name I must write the check?".

" Write the check in the name of Uduvil Handy Senior's home. I never expected you to help me with this large amount. I will issue a receipt for it. Are you giving this donation because of our friendship Jeevan ?"

"Take it anyway," Jeevan said with a laugh.

"Thank you so much, Jeevan for the financial help."

Both stood in silence by looking into each other's eyes. Through that silence, the Rathy and Jeevan exchanged their old memories.

Rajan broke his silence and said, "Well, Jeevan it's time for us to go as you have other appointments to finish. Please get Rathy's phone number and email so that you can now contact her from Canada. "

Rathy and Jeevan exchanged their WhatsApp numbers and email IDs.

"Can I take a picture with you Rathy?" Jeevan asked.

"Of course, I need a copy of the picture you take," she said.

Rajan requested both to stand side by side. He took some pictures. Jeevan gave two copies of the photos taken by Rajan. He saw the smile on her face.

"Rajan uncle please contact Rathy after you finish all legal matters. I will pay any cost involved."

Jeevan gifted Rathy two bottles of maple syrup that he brought from Canada.

Rathi requested them to have lunch with her. The two of them sat together and talked about their old friendship. Jeevan told Rajan to have Rathy as a witness in the will. He wanted to see her again on the day he is signing the will. Rajan knew why Jeevan said that.

" No problem, Jeevan. Tomorrow morning after meeting the building construction company at the hotel we will address the Will issue. It will be read out in my office at home. I have arranged for my assistant a lawyer to be at my house at ten to sign as a witness. Rathy knows my family well. We will have lunch at my house. My wife is a good cook."

Rathy agreed to be a witness. She loved to meet Jeevan tomorrow It gave joy to Jeevan's mind. Jeevan. Rajan left the Handy Seniors home at 4 PM.

Jeevan wanted Rajan to drop him at the Bank as he wanted to change dollars.

****

CHAPTER TWENTY-TWO

THE REPORTER THILLAINATHAN

After cashing the dollars from the Bank of Ceylon Jeevan met Thillainathan at the bank. Thillainathan was two classes senior to him at the college.

Thillainathan was born in the village of Vasavilan. His father was a tobacco, land, and marriage broker. Nathan has two sisters. Nathan did not marry until the two sisters were married. Nathan is a news reporter. He earned his living by writing speeches for politicians and reporting to a local newspaper.

During the period Jeevan was a student at Medical College, Nathan was collecting news from villages in Valikamam for a newspaper in Colombo. Nathan can speak and write English and Tamil well. After Jeevan moved to Colombo, he did not have any contact with Nathan for a long time. It was a surprise for Jeevan to meet Nathan. Nathan's Hitler's mustache has not changed. Nathan did not have the character of Hitler. He has a democratic policy.

It has been a long-standing culture among the Valikamam people to give a title to the villagers. For example. Kanchan Ganapati, Karuval Kandiah, Kattai

Sivarasa, Dosa Visalatchi , Minor Maniyam, Koothu Lingam, Overseer Nataraja. Thillainathan got the title Reporter Nathan.

*****

"Hello Nathan, can you remember me ?" asked Jeevan.

He replied after a few seconds " Why not? You are Dr. Jeevan, son of late Mudaliyar Murugesu ."

. " You are right Nathan. I am glad that you have a good memory. ".

" Jeevan, Chunnkam people said you migrated to Canada after working as a doctor in Colombo. Am I right?

"Yes Nathan, I emigrated to Canada after the 1983 riots "

"Good decision you took. You would have grown crazy if you had worked here"

"That's right Nathan. Have you stopped your reporter job? Have you authored any books? "Jeevan asked.

"Yes, I authored a book about some of the villages in Valikamam and the people who live there. The title of the book is Known about your Village. About seven hundred copies I printed. "

" What is the book about?"

" It is about the villages in Valigamam and the heritage, culture, and traditions of the people and about how the village got its name. Also, about temples, Schools, and important people who lived there."

"Good creativity Nathan. Give me a few copies of the book you wrote about those villages. I will take the books to Canada and give them to associations run by the Valikamam people. The members of that association will love to read it."

"I will give. How many copies do you want?"

" Please give me ten signed copies."

Nathan gave ten signed copies to Jeevan

Jeevan gave Nathan five thousand rupees.

" Dr. Jeevan, why are you paying me?"

" This is my appreciation of your research work and the cost involved in producing the book. It is a valuable book," said Jeevan.

"Thank you very much Jeevan, you are like your father Mudaliyar Murugesu. He had the habit of helping Chunnakam and other villagers. "

"Tell me how few villages got their Names."

" To start with Chunnkam, in the past the village was covered with forests. Peacocks roamed in those forests. Hence the original name was Mailini which means the land of a peacock. Even now some temples in Chunnkam carry that name. The name got changed to Chunnkam during the British time as they found limestone in that area.

The Village Alavetty was named as their paddy fields are in the wetland. It may be that a canal called the Valukai river, the second river in the Jaffna peninsula flows through this village. It is not a river, as per researchers. It is a canal that was built from a Tank in Mallakam and flows sixteen miles down the slope towards Jaffna Lake and falls near the Araly. So was the Thondamanaru that was built by Chola commander Thodaman to transport salt from Navatkuli to be sent to South India. Then you know about Mavitapuram The area where princes changed their horse-like faces to normal faces. One of the leading ports in the Jaffna peninsula is the Kankesanthurai port in the North. It got its name as the statue of Kaankeyn was brought from south India and a temple was established in Mavittapuram.

One of the five Iswarams, the Naguleswaram was established in the Valigamam area. There is a pond near the temple. It is called Keerimalai, The Temple and the and got the name from mongoose that roamed once a forest in that area."

"Have you written Nathan about any Tamil poets who lived in these villages?"

" Why not. There were many poets such as Maathgal Poet. Chunnkam Mailvaganam poet, Mahakavi from Alavetty. Somasundaram poet from Navaly, Kalladi Velan from my village Vasavilan. He created cryptic poems. He fought against injustice.

There was a pond within Jaffna Municipal Council. The responsibility of protecting the fish from extinction had been handed over to a municipal guard, who wrote on a large board that no one in the pond could catch the fish He hung the board on a tree near the pond and was satisfied that he had done his duty.

One day, Kalladi Velan who was passing by, read with curiosity the text written in Tamil on the notice board that was put on the tree.

" Oh god Tamils language is being murdered by the person who wrote this notice. There is a grammatical mistake in the text. It gives a different meaning, Velan thought to himself.

He went to a store, bought fishing bait, and started fishing in the pond. The security guard who saw a man violating the rules rushed to the pond.

"Hey !, hey! Who are you the uneducated idiot? Did not read the notice in the tree? Why are you violating the rule written in that notice?

" I can fish in this pond. The text in the notice does not clearly say that I should not fish" Velan said. He explained the grammatical mistake in the text. If the text us read grammatically it permits us to do fishing in the pond."

The guard apologized to Velan and changed the notice.

The town of Mallakam is located north of Chunnakam. The name may have come from the fact that the wrestlers in the Chola battalion once lived here."

"Nathan, I was shocked to hear what you had to say about these towns

I was born in Chunnakam. I studied in Skanda but did not know how these names came to be. This is wonderful research. Writers like you are especially important to our community.

*****

CHAPTER TWENTY-THREE

THE KEERIMALAI POND

The next day Jeevan and Rajan decided to go to Naguleswaram temple and perform a pooja. Naguleswaram as informed by Nathan is one of the five Siva temples in Sri Lanka. Nakula means mongoose in Tamil. This area was once covered with bushes and mongooses roamed in that forest. Naguleswaram is located near the Keerimalai pond. Nathan also mentioned to Jeevan about the natural Pokkunai a pond north of Chunnagam. This natural pond has an under-earth link with the Keerimalai pond. When the water level rises in the Keerimalai pond, the water level in the Pokkunai pond too rises. There are legendary stories linking Ramayana with this pond

During his school days, Jeevan went swimming with his friends in Kirimalai. It is a journey of five miles via. Malayalam, Tellipalali. Mavittapuram. The Cement Factory was functioning. The Lanka Cement Factory was started in 1950 under the Department of Industry and was converted into a public corporation in 1956 and renamed Kankesan Cement Works. The factory closed production in 1991 due to the war in the north. During the operation of the cement factory, the environment was affected as ash was deposited in the trees closer to the factory.

There is a belief among the people that bathing in the pond will cure skin diseases. Jeevan was taught in the pond to swim by his friend Ravi.

Jeevan pointed out to Rajan a shop near the pond and said "Uncle Rajan, look at that old man the owner of that shop. He is related to my mother. She helped him to start that shop. Before becoming a shopkeeper, he was rowdy like Maniam."

" I remember this man as he was a criminal and went to jail for three months for assaulting a man from Navaly."

When the shopkeeper saw Jeevan he asked, " Aiyah, are you going to do some ritual? I could arrange that."

"No. I did not come to do the ritual. Do you know me Shanmugam?"

"Sorry I cannot recognize you Aiyah. Are you new to this town"?

"No. I am Dr Jeevan the son of Mudaliyar Murugesu and Nallanachiyar . You are a relation of my mother. She helped you start this shop."

" Oh yes, I remember you now. You were a little boy. Yes, your mother is my relation, When I was without a job, she helped me to start this shop.

I will never forget that help. I heard that you went to Canada as a doctor, after the riots in this country. "

"Oh, yes Shanmugam it is true. I came back to this town after forty years. How is your business progressing?"

" Business here is not easy as before. Many shops have come up. My shop is the only shop around here that takes care of the thirty-first day after the funeral called anthireshti rituals. Many customers come here to do that.

"Shanmugam Aiyah can you briefly explain these Anthireshti and Thivasam rituals for the dead person done in Keerimalai ?"

" Why not? Hindu death rituals in all traditions follow a uniform pattern drawn from the Vedas, with variations according to sect, region, caste, and family tradition. Most rites are fulfilled by the family, all of whom participate, including the children, who need not be shielded from death. Certain rites are traditionally performed by a priest but may also be performed by the family if no priest is available.

31st-Day Memorial called Anthireshti

A priest purifies and performs the rituals making one large pinda (representing the deceased) and three small, representing the father, grandfather, and great-grandfather. The large ball is cut into three pieces and joined with the small pandas to ritually unite the soul with the ancestors in the next world. The pandas are fed to the crows, to a cow, or thrown in the sea for the fish. Some perform this rite on the 11th day after cremation. Others perform it twice and after one year. Once the first ritual is completed, the ritual impurity ends. Monthly repetition is also common for one year.

One-Year Memorial ritual is called Thivasam

a priest conducts the shraddha rites in the home, offering pinda to the ancestors. This ceremony is done yearly if the sons of the deceased are alive.

The Army is still occupying some lands that belong to Keerimalai residents. They are cultivating those lands and making money. In addition, there is a hotel that has come up near the beach. They say that it is owned by three Major generals. The cement factory is not re-activated after the war in 2009. They have built a bungalow for the President,

", Shanmugam said.,

"Isn't your son Thayalan helping you ?"

Shanmugam said after being silent for a while

"He joined the Tamil Liberation Tigers of Tamil Eelam (LTTE) and died. My daughter Sumathy married a groom from Vanni. She is happy with her family in Vanni."

"What other changes have taken place in this town Shanmugam "?

" Few Sinhala families have settled here. Look at that Buddha statue. That was put up by the Army. "

"Is your wife, OK?"

"Why are you asking that, Jeevan? She has been unwell for the last one month. She must undergo surgery. I do not have cash for my wife's surgery. No one else can help me with money "

"Don't worry Shanmugam. You keep this money. You do not need to return this money to me. This will help you to cover the cost of your wife's surgery, she loves you."

"Thanks, Jeevan, for the money. You are generous like your father."

Jeevan and Rajan spent some time looking around Keerimalai village.

They both left to meet Sivalinga Swamgal.

****

CHAPTER TWENTY-FOUR

SHIVALINGA SWAMI

Shivalinga Swami knows Jeevan's father Mudaliyar Murugesu, as he worked with Murugesu in the Jaffna Kachcheri as a clerk. Now he is 90 years old. He became a Swami at the age of forty. The real name of Shivalinga Swami is Sivarasa. After he became a Swami, he retired from his job. He meditated daily. He told Jeevan's parents that their son Jeevan will become a doctor but will live in a different country. Jeevan could remember that prediction by Shivalinga swami. Jeevan also remembered swami keeping him in his lap and teaching Hindu devotional songs.

Jeevan and Rajan went to meet Shivalinga swami in a hut in Mallakam village near the Kollen Kalati Ganapati Temple. There were four disciples with him.

Rajan too met Swami several times at Murugesu's house. There was gossip among the villagers that when Swami was working in the Jaffna Kachcheri, he had a love affair with a lady typist, but it did not end in marriage as the lady whom he loved died of serious sickness. As a result of the love failure, he switched to spiritualism.

****

"Jeevan, aren't you the son of my friend Murugesu? When did you come to Chunnakam from Canada?"

" Yes, swami I am Mudaliyar Murugesu's son. You visited my home several times. You collaborated with my father in the Jaffna kachcheri "

" Yes, you were a student when I visited your house to meet your father. As I predicted, I heard that you qualified as a doctor in this country and migrated to Canada. I did not see you for many years. What brought you to see me after many years."

"Swami, how can I forget you? When I was a little boy, you used to visit our house to meet my father. You kept me on your lap and applied holy ash on my forehead and said, I will be fine." Jeevan said.

"I know that one day you will come to Chunnakam, because all the properties of your father are here, and you came to finalize matters."

"Yes, Swami. My parents have written the will in my name. I want to renovate our house and start a Seniors Home. I came to get your blessings for that project ."

" Jeevan when you came to this world you came empty-handed, and when you leave this world, you will not take anything with you. It is good to collect good karmas. I bless you on your project. Isn't that man standing next to you the lawyer Rajan? "

"Yes, Swami, I met you at Murugesu's uncle's house a few times. Bless me as well" Rajan fell at Swami's feet and got blessed.

" Jeevan tell me why you came to see me"?

"Swami, I came to ask you about the history of the temples around here.".

"I do not know about all the temples. There are many temples here. I only know about a few temples. Jeevan the most important temples here are Naguleswaram in Kirimalai, Mavitapuram Kandasamy, Maruthadi Pillaiyar, and Innuvil Parajasekaran Pillaiyar, and the five Ganesh temples that were built by the princess who built the Mavittapuram temple with the help of her lover. The richest temple is the Nallur Kandasamy temple. There are a few more temples such as Selva Sannathy, and Vallipuram, Ponnalai Vishnu temple. Vanna Veera Maha Kali Amman temple in Nallur. The sword of the king Changiliyan who ruled the Jaffna Kingdom and fought with the Portuguese is there in that temple."

" Swami my parents took me twice to Nallur temple when I was young. At that time there was only one Gopuram. My father when he was working at Jaffna Kachcheri visits very often the Nallur temple."

" There are more Gopurams now at Nallur Kandasamy temple. My guru Yogarwswami mediated from the madam place where the chariot is parked."

"Sami, there is a Kandasamy temple in Ontario now. That temple was started in a warehouse and has now has a gopuram "

"That would have cost money to build "? Sami said.

"Yes Swami, they get a tax credit and that is why they build temples and do business."

Swami narrated to Jeevan about the history of temples in Valigamam.

Jeevan recorded what Swami was narrating about templates.

"What is that tool you have Jeevan"? Swami asked.

"Swami, this is a tool that records what you say."

"I know your father had an HMV record player. He played the devotional songs by M K Thangarajah Bagavathar and M S Subbulakshmi. I too listened to those songs. The song Krishna Mukunda Murray is still in my memory. The culture and technology are changing. The villages in Valigamam have changed. The temples here have not lost the purity."

"You're right Swami. The devotees are sending money from abroad, The Kannagi temple near our house has a Gopuram and wedding hall."

Swami said, "There are about four thousand Hindu temples in Sri Lanka. The Ramayana says that Hinduism came to Sri Lanka many years ago. Buddhism, Catholic Christianity, and Islam came after Hinduism. The five Iswarams were built many thousands of years ago to protect the island from tidal waves.

Jaffna was ruled by the Aryan dynasty from the 13th century to the beginning of the 17th century. They took the throne names Pararasasekaran and Sekarasekara alternately. It is believed that the idol in this temple was named Pararasasekara Pillaiyar and the temple was called Pararasasekara Pillaiyar Temple after a king who had the throne name of Pararasasekaran. It is not known exactly why the temple got its name from this king. Inuvik is also home to the Sekarasekara Pillaiyar Temple, which bears the other throne name of the Aryan emperors.

Inuvik was an important town from the beginning of the Aryan dynasty and had a royal representative there. Inuvik is likely to have been a state-owned town as early as the 13th century.

During the reign of the King of Jaffna, there was a monastery near this temple. Visitors to the temple used it. After the capture of Jaffna by the Portuguese, many Hindu temples including the Nallur Kandasamy temple were demolished.

Mavittapuram is a historical temple. The king who ruled the Madurai in Tamil Nadu, had a daughter by the name of Maruthapuravalli. She ridiculed a sage, and she was cursed that her face will turn into the face of a horse. Her illness is not cured by all kinds of treatments. Under the guidance of Sage Santalinga, the princess came to Kirimalai from South India worshiped at the Naguleswaram Temple and bathed in the pond. Her disease was cured, and her face returned to normal.

A Chola commander who was ruling that area fell in love with her and wanted to marry her. She said that if he builds a temple for Karthikeya at Mavittapuram she will marry him. A statue of Karthikeya was brought from south India via Kankesanthurai. Sculptors and materials were brought from Madurai to build the temple and the Mavittapuram Kandasamy temple was built. This is a temple built by Chola commander Thondaman. He was the person who built the Thondaman canal to transport salt to Tamil nandu. There is a Karthikeya temple by the name Selvasanathy near the place where the Thondaman canal meets the sea."

Swami concluded by explaining briefly about some more temples.

"Thank you, Swamis it is time, for us to go."

"Wait a minute you both should have lunch with me after a prayer meeting ".

The two could not refuse his request.

After prayers, food was served on a banana leaf. After lunch, Jeevan asked,

"Swami, I would; like to donate this money to your Asramam. "

"Jeevan this donation you are giving I will go to feed poor children who come to this Asramam for prayers."

"Okay, Swami I am sending you money through Rajan to feed the poor children".

"You're like your father, Mudaliyar Murugesu. He too was good at donating to charity. May gods bless both of you a long life."

After being blessed by Swami Jeevan and Rajan left for Chunnakam

****

CHAPTER TWENTY-FIVE

VISITING THE COLLEGE

3rd Century AD Buddhists lived in the village of Kandarodai. There are Buddhist stupas in that village. Buddhists believe that Lord Buddha visited Nainatheevu and Kandarodai. Another explanation given by Archeologists is that during the Pallava dynasty, Buddhist monks from the banks of the river Amravati came here and converted many Hindus to Buddhism. The appearance of the stupas in Kandarodai is like the stupas in Amravati. People think that those Buddhist monks may have been killed by the villagers.

*****

Skandvordaya College is a college located in Kandarodai. Its history dates to the early 19th century. The college grew and from that college, many students became Doctors, Engineers, Civil Servants, Accountants, and Teachers. Dr. Jeevan is one of them. The names of the principals of the college appeared on a board. Jeevan was well among the teachers who taught him. Jeevan entered Colombo Medical College from this college.

Past students at the college who migrated to the western countries send money to expand the college. Science and Computer labs were set up. Jeevan was overjoyed to see the name of Subramaniam on a board. He was the principal during the time Jeevan was studying at that college.

Principal Subramaniam admitted in his college, the students who had been expelled from the Jaffna Hindu College for their misconduct. He disciplined them and made them enter University.

Jeevan introduced himself as an old student at the college to the principal Rajalingam.

Rajalingam said to him that he remembered Jeevan as the first student to enter medical college from Skanda. He told him that old boys' associations that are functioning in foreign countries are financially helping the college.

Jeevan gave a check to the principal for 50,000 rupees as a donation to the college. The principal issued a receipt for the money received and thanked him for the donation.,

Jeevan told him, "There is a Skandvordaya Alumni Association in Canada. I will share my experience about this visit with them when I go there. They will do whatever they can to help the college. "All the teachers applauded and expressed their happiness.

Skandvordaya College was established in the year 1894
*****

Before leaving the College, college Principal Rajalingam told him, "Dr. Jeevan, I would like to introduce you to the students.

Jeevan agreed to it. In half an hour all the students assembled in the hall. Only students over the tenth grade gathered at the assembly hall.

The principal introduced Jeevan to the students, and he spoke

"Students, Dr. Jeevan, an old student at our college who is our guest from Canada. He was the first student to enter Colombo medical college from this college. His father Mudaliyar Murugesu room was also an old student at our college. Dr. Jeevan while at college was a senior prefect. He then emigrated to Canada after the ethnic riots. He is working in Canada as a doctor, He has come to Chunnkam after forty years.

Dr. Jeevan is the President of the Alumni Association of Canada, which has about fifty members. That association has helped our college financially and the college is grateful to that association. Dr. Jeevan has donated fifty thousand rupees to our college. I invite him to say a few words to you all."

"My dear Students, I thank your college principal and you all. It is a pleasure in meeting you all. I am Dr. Jeevan. the son of late Mudaliyar Murugesu of Chunnkam. I had memories as a student when I am visiting this college after many years. Those days, I cycled to this college with my friend Ravi who captained the college cricket team He is no longer with us. This college has made satisfactory progress. I entered Colombo Medical College where I studied, became a doctor, worked in Sri Lanka, and then migrated to Ontario Canada after the riots.

Dear students, I want you all to think positively and not get discouraged if you are not successful. You must share your knowledge with others. Not everyone can go to university. Each of you has a talent, for example, you can be a writer, a mechanic, an electrician, an Actor, or a journalist. Many of you are the sons of farmers. Those who have experience in the field of High Tech, Medicine, Engineering, and Accounting are more likely to emigrate. If you happened to emigrate you should not forget your hometown and the college where you studied. Thanks for listening to my talk. If you have any questions? I will be happy to answer." Jeevan concluded his speech.

One student said, "Dr. Sir, thank you for your inspirational speech. My name is Prabhakaran. I am a farmer's son. My father is illiterate, but he wants me to study and become a doctor. I do not know if it is possible. I want to study and serve my village if I can. My relative, Dr. Mauryan, is a Cardiac surgeon in Canada. Do you know him, Sir?"

"Oh yes, I know him. He is the patron of our alumni association in Canada. Since your name is the name of a Tamil national leader did you face any problem "?

"Why not Sir. They often check me at the army Post and then look at my ID card and ask me many questions. I replied to them without arguing with them," the student said.

" I bless you that you will fulfill your father's wish".

Jeevan left the college after answering questions from students signing Autographs.

***

CHAPTER TWENTY-SIX

THE WILL

After visiting the surrounding villages Jeevan returned to the Margosa Lodge in Rajan's car The next day Jeevan had the important assignment of writing a will with lawyer Rajan and meeting with a Construction company. The will is to be signed e at Rajan's office located at home. Rajan had arranged his assistant as a witness along with Rathy Devi as requested by Jeevan. Rajan has arranged lunch at his house after signing the will.

The building contractors' meeting was to start at 9 AM at Margosa lodge conference room. The building Engineer, Architect, Quantity surveyor, and a member of the staff of the "Yarl Constructions" were there with a draft building plan for a Senior Home for review and approval.

Rajan picked up Rathydevi from Uduvil and both were there in the lodge fifteen minutes earlier than nine am.

Jeevan was happy that he could meet Rathy during the last two days during his visit to Chunnkam.

" Jeevan, while I was coming from Uduvil in Uncle Rajan's car, on my request he stopped for a few minutes at the entrance to the house you lived. I remembered coming to that house several times with my parents when I was in my teens.

The house is partly damaged with the house chimney standing there majestically. I saw the well which you often speak about the excellent quality of water. The mango and Jack Trees are not there. I saw four men clearing the bushes and fencing the land, The house is in an ideal spot as it is on the main bus route and closer to the Railway station and Post office. I saw the cemetery and the neem tree where you engraved my name along with your name and Ravi's name."

" Rathy did you go and inspect the engraving of the names?"

"Oh no. I saw the neem tree from a distance. I saw a corpse burning."

Jeevan introduced Rathy to the lodge manager. He took her around the lodge.

Rathy commented " I like the environment of the lodge. More than that you have a bullock cart to travel, a well to draw water, Raleigh bicycles too ``are available for cycling It looks as if the lodge is promoting Jaffna traditional things."

" Yes, madame the owners of this lodge are two Jaffna Tamils from England. They are business professionals."

After a two-hour meeting with Yarl construction and finalizing the building plan, Jeevan, Rathy, and Ranjan left for Ranjan's office to sign the will.

*****

Rajan as agreed picked up Jeevan at Margosa lodge at 9 AM both traveled to Handy Senior; s home at Uduvil to pick up Rathydevi

At Rajan's office, his assistant Somasundaram was waiting with the will. Rajan introduced him to Jeevan and Rathy a. Rajan read out the will that detailed the assets left by Murugesu and Nallanachiyar in the name of their only son Jeevan and how he will be starting a senior's home in that house.

" Jeevan Murugesu, do you agree with what I read out from the will?"

" Yes, I do."

" Are you ready to sign the will?"

"Yes, I am."

Rajan gave his pen to Jeevan to sign and date it in the place shown by him.

It was mentioned in the will that Jeevan has full powers to use assets for any projects he wishes to implement. It is mentioned in the will that the name of the Senior's home will be "Nalla Murugesu Seniors Home." Jeevan named the senior's home to reflect the names of his parents.

Rathy and Rajan's assistant Sivanathan signed as witnesses.

When Rathy came to know the name of the Senior; s home she said " Jeevan you have chosen the appropriate name for the Senior's home. My father would often say that your father and mother were extremely helpful to the people of Chunnakam. "

Jeevan thanked Uncle Rajan and the two witnesses and paid him by checking the legal fees for the will.

" Jeevan after signing the will. do not think that you have washed your hands with your link with Chunnkam village. In whatever country live it is recorded in the birth certificate your place of birth as Chunnakam and it cannot be changed. You will remember Chunnkam wherever you are. My mind tells me that one day your children will come to this village. At that time there will be more change and the village would have turned formed into a town or even a city. The village is always changing, people will change. roads, buildings the temples, and the attitude of the people will change In a few more years more buildings will come, and the green Farmland will disappear. The trees will vanish as Even the name Chunnakam may change who knows. All the villages in the Jaffna peninsula are undergoing these changes which are due to the migration of people. It is good for the country's economy but not good for the environment, "said Rajan.

" I do agree with what you Rajan uncle."

" What is your next plan, Jeevan? Rathy asked him.

" Rathy tomorrow morning I will be taking the train to Colombo

In Colombo and spend a few days there visiting a few places. On the way to Colombo, I will be visiting my friend Dr. Rasheed: who studied and collaborated with me."

By the time they completed signing the will, it was one pm.

Rajan s wife Shakuntala said " You all must be feeling hungry by now. The food is ready. I have prepared King fish and crab curries. There is our local seafood soup.?

They all had lunch. At 4 PM they had tea and left for Uduvil to drop Rathy Devi

*****

CHAPTER TWENTY-SEVEN

GOODBYE

The next day after signing the will, Rathy went to Chunnakam station in Rajan's car to bid goodbye to Jeevan. Rajan picked up Rathy from the Senior's home at Uduvil and drove to Margosa Lodge.

Jeevan was ready after settling the hotel bill. When he saw Rathy in Rajan's car, he was happy that she has come to bid goodbye to him

Jeevan and Rathy were seated in the back seat and were enjoying talking until the car reached Chunnkam station

Rathy and Jeevan were left to talk alone until the train arrived at the station and Rajan went and sat in the vehicle

" Jeevan don't worry about the Senior's home you started. I ran your Senior's home project

It is an immense pleasure to meet you. After many years, our meeting has brought back old memories for both of you." said Rathy.

" I fully trust you Rathy. This Senior's home has revived a link between both of us t although we both live far apart."

" I want to give you a gift to you Jeevan Will you accept it ?" Rathy asked Jeevan

"What gift are you going to give me Rathy?"

"I know that it's too cold in Canada, so I'm having a sweater knitted by me as a gift from me to be given to you. My memory will often come back to you if you wear it."

Rathy gave me a blue color sweater for Jeevan.

"I did not expect this gift from you. It is an f gift fantastic gift. I assure you that this sweater will be in my body.

I would also like to give you a gift in return to you. During my school days, my father gave me an expensive Parker 51 pen with my name written on it. I want to give you this pen as my gift to you. You will remember when you use it," said Jeevan.

"Thank you, Jeevan for your gift. Good competition between our prizes," Ratty said with a smile.

There was an announcement that the train to Colombo is arriving in a few minutes.

"Okay, it is time to bid goodbye to both of you," Rajan said.

Jeevan and Rathy embraced and bid goodbye with tears in their eyes.

Rajan also bid hood bye to Jeevan. He asked him to call him before he takes the flight to Canada.

While driving to the Handy seniors home in Uduvil, Rajan said "Rathy now you have taken a big responsibility to establish and run the NallaMurugesu senior's home. Do not hesitate to call me if you need any help.

" Rajan Uncle I have no problem I have taken charge of the Jeevan's nursing home where I will make sure it is run with the highest efficiency. It is my duty."

Rajan dropped Rathy in Uduvil and went home.

****

CHAPTER TWENTY-EIGHT

DR. RASHEED

The morning express train from Chunnkam to Colombo left the station at the scheduled time. It is about a two hundred miles journey to Kurunegala. It takes about five hours with a stop at a few major stations. He expected to reach Kurunegala at noon. Jeevan has already informed Dr. Rashid about his visit. Rajan wanted to spend a day with his friend's family and leave for Colombo by a Taxi the next day from Kurunegala.

He did not want to stay in Colombo for more than three days. In Colombo, he planned to meet with doctors Amarasekara and Wickramanayake, who lectured him at the Medical College in Colombo. These two lecturers were very friendly with him at medical college.

****

The train arrived on schedule time and Jeevan got on the train. At 7.05 the train left the station. The Train stopped for five minutes at Jaffna station.

It stopped at major stations and reached Kurunegala at noon.

*****

.Dr. Rashid and his son Hassan were there at Kurunegala station to receive Jeevan

Kurunegala is a major city in Sri Lanka. It is the capital city of the Northwestern Province and an ancient royal capital for 50 years, from the end of the 13th century to the start of the 14th century. It is the meeting point for the raid from Colombo to Anuradhapura and Puttalam to Kandy. It is about ninety-four kilometers from Colombo, forty-two kilometers to Kandy, and fifty-four kilometers from Puttalam.

Kurunegala has been named after the Elephant rock. "Kurune" means tusker or an elephant with protruding teeth and *gala* in Sinhala means rock. *Kurenai* means tusker or an Elephant and *gal* in Tamil means rock or hill.

That night, Jeevan stayed at Dr. Rashid's home. Rashid's father worked against the ruling government, the government imposed some unnecessary baseless charges on him and kept him in solitary confinement for months. Rashid said he could not sue her and then quit his job in the government and worked in Dubai for a while, after which he finished telling his tragic story that he had returned to his hometown.

Jeevan said, "Dr. Rashid, you are not the only Sinhala government here, Tamil. Muslim doctors act because of upper extremity sex and make them hate the profession they do. As a result, many intellectuals emigrated from Sri Lanka. I am one of them. I inquired about the many Sinhala doctors who collaborated with us and learned that some of them had emigrated.

Dr. Rashid's son and daughter faced problems at school. Even Dr. Rashid's wife Ameena was treated badly by some Sinhalese teachers. Rashid told his friend Jeevan he was politically victimized by the government after the Easter Sunday attack. Some Sinhalese doctors who were jealous of his talent, instigated the hatred towards him as he belonged to the Muslim community. They went to the extent of influencing a few Singhalese women that Dr. Rasheed sterilized them It was proved as a false complaint, Jeevan had lunch and dinner at Rashid's house. Mutton biryani with Wattalappam was served for lunch. Rasheed took his friend to the Elephant rock and the lake and narrated the heritage. He also told him that Kurunegala was ruled for a brief period by a Muslim king. He was murdered by Buddhist people.

****

CHAPTER TWENTY-NINE

AT COLOMBO

The next day morning Jeevan left for Colombo via Polgahawella in a rental car arranged by his friend Dr. Rashid. . He traveled on Kurunegala Colombo Road. The road is well upgraded. He passed through Polgahawella, a major Rail route junction for Northern and upcountry lines. The etymology of the village name is a farm of coconut palms.

Many years ago, Jinadasa's used to be the go-to place you just had to stop off at on a trip between Colombo and Kandy. They used to make the best "Thala gull" (a sweet made with sesame seeds and jaggery). Now years later the legend and name remain due to what was once, but the level of the food and famous Thala guli quality tastes excellent. Locals will still recommend the place Now it is just another roadside rest shop. Jeevan bought special Thala guli sweets at Jinadasa shop in Warakapola. He ate hoppers at a shop in Nitambuwa. He is familiar with that Appuhamy hopper shop owned by an old man.

The driver asked Jeevan,

"Sir, have you ever been from Colombo to Kandy by car?"

Jeevan laughed and told him, "I have been driving many times. Many years back I was a doctor at the Kandy hospital

'Whenever I drive from Colombo to Kandy, I stop at Warakapola to buy sweets and Nitambuwa and have hoppers at Appuhamy's hopper shop. The shop is famous for Kittul hopper ."

" It looks like you still remember those two shops."

Jeevan smiled and said "That was a long time back, but these two shops have grown big now.

The boss of this Nitambuwa hopper shop used to greet everyone. He was a bearded old man with a smiling face. I remember his name was Appuhamy. I do not see him now.
"

The driver said, "He's dead. His son runs the store."

Jeevan asked the driver "Do you know about the building called Ambalama near Kadugannawa bend"?

"Yes sir. I have been several times to that building a taking tourist there," the driver replied

" Do you know the heritage of that building?"

" No sir. If you know about let me know ."

"Kadugannawa Ambalama is a historic resting place - a few meters before the Kadugannawa bend. It was built by the British during the early 19th century. Ambalama is now more than two hundred years old. A popular parking place for traveling cavalrymen and merchants, Ambalama, the structure resembles Kandy-era architecture and is of archaeological value. "

After talking to the driver, Jeevan reached Colombo.

. After reaching the hotel Galadhari, Jeevan gave the Taxi driver a few rupees more than the arranged amount.
*****

When Jeevan was in Galadhari Hotel in Colombo,

Jeevan hired a three-wheeler through the Hotel reception. Bandusena was the name of the Three-wheel driver. He was conversant with all three languages.

" Sirs call me Bandu. My hometown is Galle. I studied as St Aloysius college Galle."

" You are being a Sinhalese; how could you speak Tamil and English."

"I learned Tamil through my Muslim friends who studied with me at College One of the Burger teachers at college helped me to learn English ."

" Why is it that you did not continue with your studies"

" Poverty at home is the main reason. My father was a member of JVP. He was killed in the 1971 rebellion. Hence, I became a tourist guide. After working as a guide in Galle I moved to Colombo.

Here I am running a rented three-wheeler."

he visited the Professors Dr. Wickramanayake and Dr. Samaranayake who taught him at the Medical College.

Dr. Samaranayake could not immediately identify Jeevan as he was a student a few decades ago. Later, he identified Jeevan and hugged and expressed his happiness to see him after a long time. Dr. Samaranayake told Jeevan that his wife died two years ago, and his son is an engineer who emigrated to Australia, although his son wanted him to come and live with him in Australia, he did not want to leave his ancestral house He is happy to live comfortably in Dehiwala. , Frequently he and his friends play bridge at his home, He has a servant who does the cooking and keeps the house clean. Every day he goes for a walk with his friends on the beach. Jeevan had lunch with Dr Samaranayake . Jeevan enjoyed Rambutan Durian fruits serve as desert.

The next day in Colombo, he visited Kollupitiya, Bambalapitiya, Wellawatta and Dehiwala. At Wellawatte he went to the house at number 54 where he rented a room and studied at Medical College. That house is now replaced by a three-story building. It serves as a lodge. During his days at medical college, he had breakfast at a restaurant called Gandhi Lodge. That restaurant is no longer there. A hotel has appeared in that location, He could not spot any Morris Minor,

Volkswagen taxis. Now they are replaced by three-wheelers, because of the high petrol price,

Jeevan went to the Medical College where he studied. He could not identify the college which was once a heritage building. Now new buildings have come up in that location. The place which was once called Lipton Cairn now carries the same. At the near location, Devadagaha Muslim Mosque is still there.

The three-wheeler driver Bandu drove him to the Viharmahadevi Devi park. located opposite the Colombo Municipal council.

"The Colombo Town Hall is the Colombo City Hall, the headquarters of the Colombo Municipal Council and the office of the Mayor of Colombo. Sri Lanka is the meeting place for the elected Municipal Council members.

In 1921 the famous Scottish city planner, Professor Patrick Cades, suggested that a large central and decent municipal building be built to house the council, a public reception hall, the mayor's office, and the public library. The Colombo Public Library was established in 1925

The foundation stone for the City Hall was laid on 24 May 1924 by the Mayor of Colombo, Thomas Reid, CCS, and four years later 9 August 1928 by Governor Sir Herbert Stanley.

The driver of the three-wheeler updated Jeevan about the changes in the sites The driver functioned as a tourist guide for Jeevan

The driver took him to Galle Face. The place was once green and now the greenery is no longer there. The place has turned into a demonstration area. There were placards asking the President to resign and go home. The impact of the rising cost of living is reflected in the texts written on the boards in all three languages.

The three-wheel driver Bandusena said,

"Sir the country has gone to dogs. The people regret electing the present President. He was once a General in the army. He manipulated and staged an attack on an Easter Sunday and came to power. The Buddhist clergy supported him. Now they have realized their mistake. It is too late as the damage was done by the President. People now want him to go home ."

"Bandu, I see a lotus-type building and the Colombo Port city. Has it started functioning?"

" Sir please ask me about this pathetic story. The government was taken a good ride by the Chinese government. The present government started an Airport and Harbor down south in Hambantota. It is not an economically viable project. It is not generating revenue for the country. Few ships are only ho to that harbor. No flights from that Airport. China gave them a loan. Now the government is finding it difficult to pay interest and the loan. At that stage, the government started this Port City and Lotus tower project again taking a loan from China. The government thought that Port City will become another trade center like Dubai and Singapore. This project has affected the traders in the Pettah area. The top politicians got commissions from these projects. News media says that the political dynasty invested the dollars earned through commissions in the western world. We blamed Britishers for swindling the island. Now the Sri Lankan politicians swindled the country, which is why we are in this economic situation." Badu said angrily.

This iconic and colonial-style Galle face hotel stood there facing Galle face green. The hotel was built in 1864. It features a spa and a saltwater pool with lounge chairs that face the vast Indian Ocean.

With hardwood floors, most rooms at Galle Face Hotel offer views of the Indian Ocean, Galle Face Green, or Colombo City.

Galle Face Hotel is a 15-minute drive from a shopping mall and just twenty-two miles from Colombo International Airport. Galle

The old British-era buildings such as the Khan Clock Tower. Statham Street, the Clock Tower in Cargills, and Colombo port are still there. The old Parliament building that was built during the British period was there with a majestic look.

Bandu said that he had come to Colombo from Galle a town in the south. He came in search of work in Colombo he contracted a Muslim businessman who rented out three-wheelers. I rented a three-wheeler and paid him a percentage of his income."

Jeevan was proud to think of Bandusena's endeavor as he said he planned to buy a three-wheeler of his own in a year.

" It is not the way you think Sir. Ethnic and Religious policy by the latest politicians is used to deceive the people living in poverty."

"Bandu, what you say is true. One of my two friends I knew from the time I was studying was from Kandy and the other was from Negombo. The other was a Catholic from a fishing family whose parents were converts during the Portuguese rule. During the approximately 450 years of Portuguese, Dutch, and British rule in Sri Lanka and the British rule, they made many changes in the society but one thing I do know is that later they established the system of service here in London very well. The Ceylon Civil Service, popularly known by its abbreviated CCS, was the primary civil service of the Government of Sri Lanka under British colonial rule and immediately after independence. Established in 1833, it functioned as a part of the administrative administration of the country at various levels until Sri Lanka gained autonomy in 1948. Until its abolition in 1963, it functioned as a permanent bureaucracy or secretariat for civil servants that assisted the government.

CCSs became the Sri Lanka Administrative Service (SLAS), which incorporated all executive boards, including the CCS Officers 'and Divisional Revenue Officers' Service, with five standards.

They also set up railroads to bring upland tea to Colombo for export, as well as railways for transportation from other towns, as well as roads and concerts but in administrative high positions. There were only whites in the police. It is difficult for Tamils , and Muslims to get a high office.

"Let me tell you something, sir?"

"Ok, Bandu tells me what you want to say."

"My Jeevan listened to the Bandusena.

"Only now does the Sinhalese understand that the LTTE leader is a genius? They fought against this government for more than 30 years. They established an Army; the Navy and the Air Force had a suicide squad.

The JVP does not have anything like that before in 1971 rebellion. They depend only on the village Sinhalese youth in the south.

If the government would have fought face to face with the LTTE, they would have certainly failed.

I know that more than twenty-two countries helped the Sri Lankan government. India, Pakistan, China, and the United States, why did so many Western countries help? They gave weapons. It became a big loan to be paid back. That is one of the many reasons for the present state of the Economy.

I do not want to talk to you too much about this because what many people know is that international politics is a complicated politics where superpowers are involved.

The only fear that came to India was that if the LTTE wins the war, Tamil Nadu would become a country along with Northeastern and Eastern Province. That was the fear that they worked against the LTTE," said Bandu.

"Bandu, what you are saying is true. Many of my Sinhala friends have also said that this problem would not have existed. Successive governments that were in power used the ethnic discriminatory policies to come to power. They painted a bad picture of Tamils and Muslim communities among the rural Singhala masses. Now the people have realized their mistake. This divide and rule policy cannot continue anymore."

It was a great surprise for Jeevan to observe that a Sinhalese youth would speak like this about ethnic unity. It means that a Transition is taking place not only in his village but in the entire country.

****

CHAPTER THIRTY

THE JOURNEY BACK TO CANADA

After spending three days in Colombo, Jeevan boarded a Sri Lankan Airlines flight from Colombo to London. His expectation that the political and economic situation of the island would have excelled was a disappointment.

He met a Singhala customs officer who was checking his badges, His name on the badge in his uniform appeared as Ramanayake.

After checking his baggage and passport, he said " Dr. Jeevan

Did you enjoy your stay on this island? You have not bought anything other than a Batik shirt, A devil Mask, a brass lamp, some sweets, and a Saree."

" I did enjoy my stay in my village in Jaffna peninsula. It has changed. Many cultivable lands are used for buildings. I did meet a few of my friends, but in Colombo, I saw many protests about the prohibitive cost of living. It looks as if people are very unhappy with the government. I also noticed that few foreign tourists at the Airport. I am taking the items you mentioned to my wife, son, and daughter."

" As a government official, I cannot give my comments on what you said. Foreign tourist arrivals have indeed declined. In short, things are getting worse after independence on this beautiful island. I do not know where the island is moving towards." Ramanayake replied.

Jeevan waited for half an hour for the call for boarding. After passing the security check he boarded the plane.

****

On the flight to London Jeevan met two Tamil families.

One of them was a Tamil traveling to London. The other is a Tamil family traveling to Germany. One Tamil said that the reason for his emigration is that they cannot any longer live in Sri Lanka. The economy is collapsing, and the cost of living is increasing. Violence and political revenge are prevailing in all sectors, "said one traveler desperately.

The other Tamil himself was a sub-editor of a newspaper that authored articles that are critical of government policies. The CID was looking for him to arrest under the Prevention of Terrorism act.

He managed to escape with the help of a businessman.

"What is your opinion on the involvement of Buddhist monks involving in politics?" Jeevan asked him,

"The preaching of Lord Buddha is not being followed in Sri Lanka and the government came to power with the support of Buddhist monks. The monks are responsible for instigating the majority against the minority communities. The government did not like what I wrote about in the paper. I said that Sri Lanka is misusing the independence given by the British. The island is now getting involved in international politics. China, India, and the domination of the West have affected this country.

"Which university did you go to?" Jeevan asked.

He said, "I studied at the University of Peradeniya, and did a degree in political science and then worked in the field of journalism and worked as a newspaper assistant editor ."

Jeevan knew that few media men were murdered by the gangs who were working for the government.

Jeevan asked about giving him his business card. He refused to give.

The reason is that Jeevan understood, Jeevan gave his business card and spoke

"If you come to Canada, come and meet me. I will do what you can to help you."

He thanked Jeevan.

"I have always known the politics of Sri Lanka through YouTube. When I came to Sri Lanka, I prayed that there should be no ethnic riots," Jeevan said.

To which he said, "Many intellectuals in Sri Lanka like you have emigrated. The people who are left behind in the country engage in corruption, crimes, and human rights violations.

Jeevan also endorsed his opinion.

After two hours in London, Jeevan took the Air Canada flight to Toronto. Jeevan's wife and two children were at the Toronto Pearson International Airport to receive him.

After hugging Jeevan, Malini said, " Jeevan, I a thank God that you did not face any problems during your stay in that country."

" Malini, I spent most of my time visiting friends and places

in the Valigamam area. I spent a day in Kurunegala and two days in Colombo. I noticed that people are protesting about the high Cost of Living. My observation is that there may be a people's revolution like the French revolution.

People say that a political family has swindled the country."

" Have you settled your will issues?"

"Yes, Malini I have set the ball rolling on my Senior home project. If the economic situation gets worsened, I may delay the project or in the alternative, I may sell my assets," replied Jeevan.

***

CHAPTER THIRTY-ONE

UNEXPECTED DECISION

NallaMurugesu Seniors Retirement Home at Chunnagam which was started a year ago was doing well. Rathy, who manages the Retirement home, has been in touch with Jeevan monthly and has been reporting to him how the Retirement home is doing. It was also an opportunity for Rathy to be in constant touch with her ex-lover.

Malini, Jeevan's wife at times talks to Rathy. She is impressed by the polite way Rathi speaks to her. She once told Jeevan " Rathy appears to be a better partner to you than me."

Jeevan avoided replying to her comment. In his heart, he accepted Malini's comments.

Rathy spoke in English with Jeevan's two children. They too started to like her. Rathy insisted they come to Chunnagam with their parents.

The Senior's Retirement home, which initially started with twenty people, has grown into a nursing home with fifty people in two years. The staff in the home contained a retired doctor, two nurses, two assistants, and two cooks. Expatriate Tamils from Valigamam who live in Canada,

London, Australia, Switzerland, and France provided financial assistance to the Senior's home.

A senior businessman named Thangarajah applied to join the Senior's home.

Rathy as Manager of the Seniors home wanted to know if he satisfies the conditions to be admitted.

"Thangarajah Aiyah, you have applied to join this old age home. Which is your hometown?" Rathi asked.

"I was born in Tellipalali. I did business in Colombo. I had an only daughter Vasanthy who got married and after a long time gave birth to a granddaughter Malathy. When my granddaughter was two years old my daughter and son-in-law died in a car accident. Raising my granddaughter has come under my responsibility.

I thought about what to do for my granddaughter to grow up better in an orphanage. That orphanage is in the Vanni area. I cannot see her often. That is why I applied here," said Thangarajah.

When she heard his story, Rathy felt sorry for him and his granddaughter.

Knowing how much Thangarajah loved his granddaughter. He wanted his granddaughter closer to him. Rathy decided to find a solution to resolve his problem.

Rathy lived alone in an outhouse next to the Senior's home.

All her expenses were paid by the NallaMurugesu Senior's home project. After reviewing Thangrajah's problem, Rathy produced a solution.

She told him, "Thangarajah Aiyah you deserve to be in this nursing home. At the same time, you do not want to be separated from your granddaughter Malathy. I understand the problem of visiting her in the Vanni if she is admitted to Childers's home in Vavuniya town in Vanni."

" Yes, Ammah. I will donate half of my hard-earned assets to this Senior's home. I will write the balance of my assets for my granddaughter and that is all I can do. "

"It's your choice. but should I know your main aim is that you wish to stay closer to your granddaughter? Am I right?"

"Yes, Ammah. If you have a solution to resolve my problem, I will be too happy," said Thangarajah

"In that case can I adopt your granddaughter? I will take care of her like my daughter. I am not married. I will educate her and guide her."

The old man did not expect that answer. "You are a God-given angel to me. I am incredibly happy to hear your advice."

" But one condition Aiyah. I will talk to my friend Dr. Jeevan and his family and get their consent and I will let you know his opinion

is. That family built this Senior's home, " said Rathy.

"It's okay for me, I heard that there is a close friendship between you and Dr. Jeevan who is the founder of this NallaMurugesu senior's home."

" I will give him a tomorrow and explain to him his family about your case. They may agree ."

The old man said, "Please talk to the doctor, and let him and his family take a decision I have no objection to your suggestion to adopt my granddaughter."

The next day Rathy spoke to Dr. Jeevan and his family on WhatsApp and explained to them about her plan to adopt a child who lost her parents. She also said to them that her grandfather, a former businessman is willing to donate half his assets to the Senior's home and the other half to his loving granddaughter.

After hearing what Rathy said, Dr. Jeevan was surprised to hear Rathy's decision to adopt a child.

Jeevan's wife Malini said, "Jeevan, Rathy is a different kind of lady. It is difficult to find what is in her mind. Once she takes a decision, she will not change from it. You to behave like her. This is my opinion after talking to her. She was your friend from your school days. If you are married to her, you may have served the community even better. But it is the fate that decided the marriage between us She is determined not to marry after she failed love affair ."

"Let us not talk about the past. We cannot change her decision. It is a good decision for her to adopt a child. When Rathy gets old, the child will look after her. I never expected her to take this brave decision. She also told me that the assets that were left behind by her parents will go to this child. I will tell Rathy and inform her that myself and my family are in total agreement with her decision to adopt Malathy, Thangrajah's granddaughter. Uncle Rajan will sort out all legal issues associated with Rathy adopting Malathy. I will speak to Uncle Rajan and give our family approval for Rathy's decision.

In a month after clearing all legal hurdles Malathy became their daughter of Rathy and started living with her in the outhouse. Since Malathy showed interest in music Rathy arranged for a teacher to teach her violin. Rathy admitted her to Uduvil girls' school. Rathy was determined to see that Malathy becomes a doctor and serves Valigamam villages.

Thangarajah had the opportunity to meet his granddaughter Malathy frequently. He took her for a walk in the park behind the senior's home.

One day he asked Malathy " Do you like your mother Rathy?"

" Of course. I love her very much. She cares for me. We have meals together. She teaches me English. She told me that she was an English teacher at Uduvil girl's school where I study."

" Did you ask her about who is your father?"

"Rathy Ammah told me the entire story about me. She also told me that my parents died in a car accident, and I am her adopted child. She never hides things, grandpa," Malathy replied to him with a smile.

Thangarajah heard the rings of the Kannagi Amman temple bells.

The end

****

Glossary Of Terms

Aachi – Old lady

Aiyah - Equivalent to Sir.

Aiyar – A Hindu priest.

Ambalama - Resting place.

Ambalama – A resting place for travelers

Ammi, Ural, Sullagu, Ulakkai, Adupu, Aatu Kal – Cooking instruments.

Anthireshti - 31st day Hindu ritual for a dead person.

Cheetu – The Chit fund .

Galle – A town in the southern province.

Karuthakolumban – A popular variety of mango

Kattu Sambol - A Sri Lankan dish made from chilies

Kiduku- Used for roofing and fencing

Kurunegala – Town in Sri Lanka

Mudaliyar - Honorary title is given during the British period

Panchamars – They are also called Kudimagans. House helpers.

Seeni Sambol - A Sinhalese food prepared from onions.

Thala guli – A sweet made from jaggery.

Thula - A lever system to draw water from the well.

Thivasam – Annual Hindu ritual for a dead person

Wattalappam - A Sri Lankan desert.

Wallowa- A bungalow on a ranch of many acres.

www.ingramcontent.com/pod-product-compliance
Lightning Source LLC
Chambersburg PA
CBHW021203130726
47988CB00002B/486